CW00505936

Eric Ambler was born into a far[...] early years helped out as a puppetee[...] engineering as a full time career, alth[...] writing. In World War II he entered t[...] and looked likely to fight in the line, but was soon after commissioned and ended the war as assistant director of the army film unit and a Lieutenant-Colonel.

This experience translated into civilian life and Ambler had a very successful career as a screen writer, receiving an Academy Award for his work on *The Cruel Sea* by Nicolas Monsarrat in 1953. Many of his own works have been filmed, the most famous probably being *Light of Day*, filmed as *Topkapi* under which title it is now published.

He established a reputation as a thriller writer of extraordinary depth and originality and received many other accolades during his lifetime, including two *Edgar Awards* from *The Mystery Writers of America* (best novel for *Topkapi* and best biographical work for *Here Lies Eric Ambler),* and two *Gold Dagger Awards* from the *Crime Writer's Association (Passage of Arms* and *The Levanter).*

Often credited as being the inventor of the modern political thriller, *John Le Carre* once described Ambler as '*the source on which we all draw.*' A recurring theme in his works is the success of the well meaning yet somewhat bungling amateur who triumphs in the face of both adversity and hardened professionals.

Ambler wrote under his own name and also during the 1950's a series of novels as *Eliot Reed*, with *Charles Rhodda*. These are now published under the '*Ambler*' umbrella.

Works of **ERIC AMBLER** published by
HOUSE OF STRATUS

DOCTOR FRIGO
JUDGMENT ON DELTCHEV
THE LEVANTER
THE SCHIRMER INHERITANCE
THE SIEGE OF THE VILLA LIPP   (Also as 'Send No More Roses')
TOPKAPI   (Also as 'The Light Of Day')

Originally as Eliot Reed with Charles Rhodda:
CHARTER TO DANGER
THE MARAS AFFAIR
PASSPORT TO PANIC
TENDER TO DANGER   (Also as 'Tender To Moonlight')
SKYTIP

Autobiography:
HERE LIES ERIC AMBLER

Tender to Danger

'Tender to Moonlight'

eric Ambler

(Writing as Eliot Reed with Charles Rhodda)

HOUSE OF
STRATUS

This edition published in 2009 by House of Stratus, an imprint of
Stratus Books Ltd., 21 Beeching Park, Kelly Bray,
Cornwall, PL17 8QS, UK.

www.houseofstratus.com

A catalogue record for this book is available from the British Library and the Library
of Congress.

ISBN 0-7551-1767-0
EAN 978-0-7551-1767-3

Prologue

MR. MERIDEN was eccentric. Mr. Meriden was very rich. Mr. Meriden was very stubborn. He was also a very tiresome man. Untroubled either by a sense of humour or by too keen an awareness of reality, he pursued his eccentricities with a determination that had something quite obsessional about it. No obstacle deterred him; no obstacle, that is, which could be battered down by money. Opposition to his wishes merely confirmed his belief in the essential rightness of them. Those who worked for Mr. Meriden earned their pay.

The Skipper of the motor yacht *Moonlight* thought of all this as he gazed across the green water of Zavrana's little harbour. When he looked at the mountains that drew an ominous curtain round the town, he remembered his mild protest against the voyage. "Well, I don't know, Mr. Meriden. Supposing there's a war. Yugoslavia's a long way from home."

War! Mr. Meriden had smiled omnipotently and laid it down that there would be no war, and here they were, idling along the Dalmatian coast through the sunny August of 1939.

They had spent three weeks among the islands between Dubrovnik and Split, and had put back to Zavrana because of a rumour that a peasant had ploughed up a bust of Diocletian and was prepared to consider any reasonable offer. Mr. Meriden had been disappointed. Inquiries on the spot had discovered neither peasant nor emperor, and to console himself Mr. Meriden had bought a palace in the hills. He had not waited to ask himself what he wanted with a palace on the Dalmatian coast. There it had been, onion-domed turret and all, and really quite cheap when you considered. Mr. Meriden had promptly entered a new cloud-cuckoo land. He saw himself established in ducal state; but democratic, the little father of his retainers, wearing the native costume; and if there weren't a native costume, he would design one.

Now he was in love with this new fantasy, and Zavrana played into it admirably. Nothing could be more serene than the lovely islands that floated in the blue reaches of the Adriatic beyond. The broken reflections of lean masts and drying sails turned lazily in the green water of the port. The tinted roofs of pleasant, but not palatial, villas were visible on the wooded foothills amidst the oaks and chestnuts, the cypresses and cedars of Lebanon. There were orangeries and olive groves and the glittering, cycloramic backdrop of the Dinaric Alps to lend its enchantment to Zavrana itself, nestling (cosiness figured prominently in Mr. Meriden's fantasy) snugly in the foreground. It was the ideal base, picturesque, secluded, blissfully quiet, and with Dubrovnik easily accessible by car. Its one small enterprise combined the functions of boatyard and undertaking establishment. The work was cheap and good, whether you wanted a coffin or a dinghy. Mr. Meriden had looked at a design for a coffin, but had decided that it could wait awhile, even though the quotation was very favourable. He had crossed to the other department and discussed some work to be done on the yacht. There had been storm damage to be repaired; also he had wanted alterations in the saloon. He had found he could save lots of dinars on the estimate those Dubrovnik sharks had given him. And then, a wonderful thing had happened. He had found another bargain.

The Skipper lowered his eyes from the Bosnian uplands and focused his binoculars on a small yawl-rigged craft that had been drawn up on the shingle of the boatyard. A few days ago two youngsters had brought her in to Zavrana, completing a holiday voyage from Plymouth. The yawl, too, had suffered storm damage and was being repaired. The Skipper had cast approving eyes upon her, observing her nice rig and her admirable lines; but now, as he peered through his binoculars, he scowled at her. She had suddenly become an impediment, a responsibility heaped upon all his other responsibilities, and heaven knows, there were enough of them.

For once, exasperation had blotted out the lessons of experience. He had had the temerity to protest vigorously.

"But, Mr. Meriden, she's thirty foot with a nine-foot beam! How do you suppose we're going to handle her?"

"We shan't have to handle her." Mr. Meriden had produced his omnipotent smile. "I'll keep her here, mainly. She'll be more than useful when I'm in residence up there." He waved negligently towards the far-off onion dome that peeped above a line of trees, then focused on the yawl again. "She's got an auxiliary. If necessary, she can follow us round. She's just the thing we want to fetch and carry when we can't tie up."

"Isn't the launch good enough, Mr. Meriden?"

"That last Greek statue we bought nearly sank the launch."

The Skipper had groaned. He had foreseen a manifest of bigger if not better pieces of marble. He had plunged on.

"I wonder if you're wise, sir. I hear she was leaking quite badly when she came in."

"They're fixing her timbers. In a few days she'll be as right as a trivet."

Useless to cast doubt on the seaworthiness of a trivet. The Skipper had seen that argument was futile. Mr. Meriden had gone on talking.

"Anyway, I want to help those lads. They're scared of all of this war talk. I've tried to tell them there's nothing in it, but they won't listen. They want to sell, fly home, and join up. She's a lovely little craft, and a real bargain."

That had been the final word. The Skipper groaned again, blinked once, and let his binoculars swing from their strap. Very rarely had Mr. Meriden been able to resist or weigh the cost of a bargain. The *Moonlight* herself was an outstanding instance of this weakness. It had taken a small fortune to build and equip her, and she had been bought for a song only because her first millionaire owner had found it impossible to face the enormous expense of running her.

The Skipper shrugged. When he next looked at the yawl on the shingle, a man in a green sweater was painting something on her square stern.

Once more the binoculars were raised. The man in the green sweater stepped back, brush in hand, to survey his work, and the Skipper could clearly see the black lettering on the white stern.

One

A THIN MIST dimmed the lights of Brussels as the plane from Athens circled the airport and prepared to land. Dr. Andrew Maclaren, shifting in his seat, looked at his watch, then at the space outside. The plane was late. It did not matter, but he had been hoping to get to London that night; merely hoping, there was no compelling reason for him to be there.

Yet London had been more and more in his mind during the weeks of indecision about his resignation. It had become a symbol of release, a goal, something to support him in the painful moment of casting off; a symbol, too, of his break with the past and his hopes for the future. He had put in quite enough time cleaning up the aftermath of Hitler's war, hanging onto the tassels of the Iron Curtain, prescribing pills for and pumping serum into displaced persons. It was amazing to him now that he had stuck it so long. Berlin had been good practice. Vienna had been a bore. Then Greece; up in the mountains and down on the shores. Who was the displaced person?

London was home.

It might also be home for the girl who sat two seats ahead of him. He had learned at any rate that it was her destination and, curiously, he derived a lot of satisfaction from the fact, just as he had from merely watching her. They lived in the same city; they were, in a way, neighbours. It was true, she might dwell in Hendon while he must plant himself at Holland Park, but from here, flying in the mist over Belgium, London seemed a small place. Sometimes when she looked across the cabin or turned towards the window, he saw her profile. Otherwise all he could see was a glowing head of auburn hair supported by a pair of very nice shoulders. It was the profile that had attracted him. It was a profile that might attract any man. Her name was ...

"I am afraid, Herr Doktor, it will be very disagreeable over the sea. Once before I was flying in a fog over the sea and I do not like it."

Mr. Kusitch leaned across to speak, fumbling with the straps of his seat. Dr. Maclaren nodded vaguely. He was annoyed with Mr. Kusitch for formulating the thought in his own mind.

"Very little to worry about," he mumbled. "With radar and beams and things, there's nothing to it."

Mr. Kusitch failed to notice the irritability in the young man's voice. His round, mournful face was as trusting as a dog's.

"You relieve me, Herr Doktor. It would be very inconvenient to spend the night in Brussels. Not that I am unfamiliar. Do you know Brussels?"

There was something of the limpet and a good deal of the bore about Mr. Kusitch. He had introduced himself before the Acropolis had been out of sight, and all the way across Europe he had chatted. He, too, was booked for London, yet Dr. Maclaren had never once thought of him as a neighbour. Mr. Kusitch was, in every stitch of his clothes, a foreigner; a foreigner with a return ticket in his wallet. An amiable little man with a pathological need for company.

The girl two seats ahead was regrettably without that need. She sat alone, an isolate. She was obviously so sure of herself, so self-contained, that it was difficult to imagine her responding to any approach from a stranger.

Her name was Miss Meriden. He had heard the air hostess address her as Miss Meriden.

"You do not know Brussels?" Mr. Kusitch was not to be ignored.

"No. I've never been in the place."

It was a mistake. Andrew Maclaren realised it at once.——"Don't be grieved, Herr Doktor. If the sad fate swallows us, I shall make it the pleasure to be your cicerone."

The wide mouth with the overhanging upper lip expanded in a smile, but the eyes were anxious, seeking reassurance from the Herr Doktor. The eyes were a cold grey, and there was something peculiar about them in addition to the slight cast in one of them. The strangeness, though, was only a momentary phenomenon, fugitive. You might even say furtive. Something looked out that should have been hidden. You decided that here were the eyes of a frank nature, pleading the honesty of their possessor. "See," they said. "This little Kusitch is a good fellow. He puts everything on the counter. There is nothing up his sleeve." Then it came: the flick of a shutter that hinted at some unnameable mystery.

It was a common peculiarity these days. Andrew Maclaren had met it frequently among the outcasts and fugitives who had been his patients. Sometimes he had known it for the mark of a concentration camp, or of some other horror endured. Sometimes its origins had remained unknown. Then it had made him uneasy, and his mind had been filled with tales he had heard of secret collaborators, of fears and betrayals, of greed and desperation more terrible than ordinary suffering.

Yet for this odd little man, Kusitch, you could surely accept one of the more innocent implications. He was a clerk, a messenger, a government servant. At most he would be the chief of some minor bureau in one of those countries beyond the Adriatic. The Slavonic suggestion in the name meant little. Mr. Kusitch could be a currant merchant from Smyrna, a tobacco salesman from Beirut, a shipping agent from Port Said. All Andrew knew was that he was a passenger from Athens to London.

"You are very kind," Andrew said, "but I don't imagine we'll see anything of Brussels. The plane will be waiting to take us on."

He was wrong. When they landed a few seconds later, the

airport officials met them with the announcement that the fog was thick over southern England and all services to London had been suspended. Andrew damned the weather. Kusitch expressed himself in what was probably his native tongue. Andrew hurried across the tarmac, looking for the girl. He had lost sight of her in the process of disembarking. She had been one of the first out, and by the time he reached the top of the gangway she had disappeared. There was a turning and milling of passengers and friends who had come to greet them. Only a few of those passengers were booked to go on; for the rest, Brussels was the end of the journey. A second plane had just arrived and there was some congestion at the passport control.

He squeezed ahead of a stout woman with a bulging suitcase.

The girl might be in difficulties. The self-assurance so manifest on the plane might not be equal to this situation. There were circumstances in which it might be no joke to be stranded in an alien city. Dubious characters were only too ready to take advantage of the lone foreigner. Now, if ever, was the time for a neighbour to keep a neighbourly eye open.

It is possible that Dr. Maclaren's prolonged acquaintance with the terrors and confusions of a vast social upheaval had induced in him a certain naïveté about the better-ordered centres. It is also possible that his capacity for self-deception had suddenly increased. The suspicion did, indeed, cross his mind that his anxiety about the girl might be related to his appreciation of her profile, but he promptly rejected it. It had been agreeable to examine that profile when he found the opportunity, agreeable to speculate on the character of its owner, to see nobility in the line of the brow, sensitivity and delicacy in the fine modelling of the nose, warmth and gentleness in the curve of the lips, firmness in that nice chin. It had been agreeable, too, to think of chances that might promote acquaintance, because he thought a man might find a good companion in such a girl; but he was not one to make a fool of himself over an attractive girl. Aesthetic appreciation was one thing, practical assistance to a distressed fellow countryman another.

So his eye was really neighbourly when a group in front of him dissolved and he saw the girl arguing with a porter. And, just as he had feared, she was in difficulty. The porter was waving his hands and shaking his head, and it seemed that she was trying to make him understand something. Now was the time to walk up and take charge of the situation, to give the man in his stammering French the order that her English could not convey to him. Yet now was the time when shyness seized Andrew, and he could not budge.

She frowned. She spoke with obvious insistence about something. The porter shrugged and waved his hands again. She seemed more disturbed, and looked round the long hall as if seeking something or someone. She needed aid. Her eyes rested upon Andrew or they looked through him, beyond him, not seeing him. For a moment he wasn't sure. Then he was. He saw appeal in her look, and, once positive, he acted on impulse. She had seen him on the plane, and now, in distress, she knew she could turn to him.

In the instant he was guiltless of opportunism. She was just another displaced person in need of assistance. He crossed the narrow space between them with assurance.

"Can I be of any help?"

Her blue eyes opened more widely in mild surprise. He was near enough to see that the profile was not an entirely adequate index of her loveliness. Or he had been too long away from her kind and saw more beauty than was there. At least one might not deny the eyes. They could be devastating.

They were. The surprise in them seemed to change to apprehension and cold suspicion. They were plainly seeing him for the first time. They were made of blue ice.

"I beg your pardon," she said.

He felt himself shrivelling. There was an eternity of horror in which he tried to think of something to say.

"I was on the plane. I thought I might be able to help you."

"Thank you," she answered. "I can manage."

She turned her back on him; then, crying a name, she ran

9

towards the far door to greet effusively an elderly fur-wrapped woman who had just entered. It was a moment before he realised that Mr. Kusitch was at his side again.

"Ah, Herr Doktor. I have found out the arrangements. They hope for resumptions to London in the morning. Seats are reserved for us on the plane at ten hours. Soon we go by autobus to the terminal building. The air people will help us with accomodations for sleeping the night."

Andrew watched the girl leave the building with the fur wrapped woman. He was almost trembling now with anger and humiliation. So that's what came of trying to help people! For his part she could sleep the night on a concrete floor.

He looked at the little man at his side and felt a twinge of compunction. Kusitch was at least human and friendly. He was talking now, gesturing towards a counter on one side of the hall. There were formalities.

Andrew recovered his humour suddenly. He laughed.

"Let's go," he said.

Mr. Kusitch beamed.

"That's right, Herr Doktor," he applauded. "For a few hours we can afford to be philosophers."

It might be that the pale grey eyes could never express the amiability of the round face. There were other thoughts in the Kusitch mind, perhaps, but what could be more natural? He was worried about some business appointment, even if he did make a pretence of shrugging it off.

He went on talking cheerfully to Andrew, but the grey eyes were quick in a flickering search, scanning the faces of those about him, the waiting passengers, the attendant friends, the air-line officials, the customs men.

In the crowded autobus it was the same, and again at the terminal building, where people passed in and out of the doors. It went on, even while he was talking to the clerk at the desk, the alert eyes peering and shifting, until Maclaren thought he must have been mistaken about the little man. He was no longer a clerk or a currant merchant. He was more like a police agent in his practised scrutiny of people. The face was impassive, or it beamed. The scrutiny was suspicious, or it might be merely curious. Andrew did not know. He had himself looked round curiously once or twice, but the red-haired hoyden was not in the terminal building, nor had she travelled in the autobus. He decided that she must have gone off somewhere with the woman in the furs, probably to dine with the royal family. The royal family was welcome. Personally he never wanted to see her again.

He felt a tug at his sleeve, and there was the faithful Mr. Kusitch, steering him towards a new counter. He detached his sleeve from the guiding grip and spoke a little impatiently. There were moments when he disliked Mr. Kusitch almost as much as he now disliked the girl, but in the case of Mr. Kusitch the feeling never had time to grow. The round, pliable face would beam again and assume the half-appealing, half-quizzical expression of the trusting dog. It was like that now.

"Leave everything to me, Herr Doktor," Mr. Kusitch said.

He found the clerk who had charge of the accomodations and spoke to him in rapid French that Andrew could follow only in part. Mr. Kusitch frowned and gesticulated. He was definitely the tobacco salesman from Beirut, and someone had offered him a bad cigar.

It seemed there was trouble. More than one or two planes had been grounded for the night, and rooms were scarce in Brussels. All this might well be, but Mr. Kusitch was not satisfied with his allocation. The hotel was bad, he said. Once he had been there. Never again. He frowned more deeply, gesticulated more wildly. If Dr. Maclaren could go to the Risler-Moircy, then he could go to the Risler-Moircy.

When Andrew understood the situation, he tried to silence the little man. They could exchange, he said. He was not particular, so long as he had a reasonable bed. Let Mr. Kusitch go to the Risler-Moircy, whatever that was.

"No, no, no!" Mr. Kusitch changed to English. "It is not thinkable that I desert you when you have my word to look after you. We travel together. We stay in the same hotel. We go forward to London together."

Andrew began to regret Mr. Kusitch altogether. He spoke a little coldly. "It's quite unnecessary. I'm used to looking after myself."

Kusitch shook his head violently. "Do not be anxious, Herr Doktor. I will fix. Leave everything to me."

"I assure you . . ."

But Kusitch had already turned to the clerk and was deep in another volley of French. He flapped a hand, palm outward, at Andrew. The clerk seemed uncertain. Kusitch leaned forward confidentially, lowered his voice to a whisper, and again indicated Andrew. At last, with an angry shrug, the clerk took up a telephone and began to speak quickly.

"What's going on here?" Andrew demanded.

"Patience," Kusitch urged. "Everything will be all right. I said it was not safe for me to be left without a friend. I told him I had the falling sickness."

Andrew stared. "Is that true?"

"In the diplomatic sense." Mr. Kusitch smiled and made a deprecating gesture.

At that moment the clerk put down the telephone and scribbled in pencil on a card. "Risler-Moircy," he read aloud. "Suite three eighteen. Okay?"

"Okay." Kusitch was severe. He took the card with only a word of thanks. But he winked at Andrew.

For a moment or two, Andrew was on the point of telling Kusitch to go off to the Risler-Moircy on his own. He had, suddenly, an acute dislike of the man. There was nothing of fear in it, nothing of premonition, only a desire to be rid of him. He halted on the pavement outside the terminal building. He hesitated, but with no sense that he had come to a moment of extraordinary decision. Then, when he heard the hooting of cars and saw the strange traffic wheeling and weaving along the strange street, he felt a weariness that was near exhaustion. His dislike faded. Kusitch might be a presumptuous bore but, at least, he had secured comfortable beds for them. That was something.

Kusitch had found a taxi and was waiting on the curb with the inviting smile of a hired guide. Andrew hesitated no longer. He stepped inside.

Two

THE RISLER-MOIRCY was after all a modest sort of family hotel with a lot of fumed oak and dark parquetry and a push-button lift that clanged and shuddered as it ascended. There was a faint smell of upholstery dust. The floor boards creaked and shifted under the parquetry, the crystal pendants of wall lamps trembled as you passed them. The Risler-Moircy's best days were done.

"It is nice," Mr. Kusitch said. "I have been here before. It is quiet, and very respectable. Nothing ever happens here."

Afterwards, for days on end, Andrew was to dredge his memory in an effort to bring back every little detail of those hours in Brussels, to recall all that he could of Mr. Kusitch: his actions, his facial expressions, his words, the inflections even with which they were uttered. But at the time Andrew's attitude towards his companion was composed of about equal parts of amusement, indifference and irritation; and some bewilderment, too.

There was, for instance, Kusitch's insistence that they should not be separated and the fact, later to become apparent, that Kusitch had asked for a suite and not merely two rooms in the same hotel. On the pretence of being an epileptic, moreover. The man seemed to make a habit of exploiting imaginary ailments to gain his ends. No doubt, if the situation had demanded it, he would have given himself bubonic plague without batting an eyelid.

The suite was the modest sort of thing you might have expected in the Risler-Moircy. It consisted of two rooms with a communicating bathroom. One of the rooms was furnished with a double bed and the customary fittings of a bedroom; the other was more like a sitting room, with a three-foot divan made up for the night. Both chambers had doors on the corridor, and there was a key for each door.

Mr. Kusitch inspected the old-fashioned locks, tried the keys in them, frowned and shrugged.

"It is best to be careful," he explained. "There are sometimes thieves in these hotels."

Andrew was indifferent. "I'm not carrying valuables. If you're nervous about anything, you can get the manager to lock it in the safe."

"No, no, no!" Kusitch was anxious to reassure his friend. "It is nothing like that. I do not care for my things to be disturbed. That is all. Also, you know, they will steal anything these days." He made a daring attempt at idiom. "I do not wish to lose my shirt."

Andrew laughed and felt better.

Kusitch inspected the windows. The one in the sitting room opened onto a narrow balcony that gave access to a fire escape. There was no such convenience for the occupant of the bedroom, whose way of retreat must be through the bathroom.

Andrew wondered if his companion was nervous about fire, also, but apparently not.

"If you do not object, I would like to use the double bed," said Mr. Kusitch carefully. "I regret that I do not offer you at once the best room, but I cannot sleep in a small bed. It is my liver complaint. It makes me restless in the night."

He looked at his companion anxiously, then added, as if he thought more persuasion was necessary: "I need large bed, or there is danger that I fall on the floor. Once I broke a bone so."

"Don't worry about me," Andrew told him. "I prefer the divan."

"It is good of you. We will wash; then I take you to a restaurant I know. The finest restaurant in Brussels for Wiener Schnitzel. And with good wine."

"We'll have to go easy. I didn't bring much emergency money."

"No matter. I have enough. You will be my guest."

"We'll see."

"No, no. It will be my pleasure. Now I will put out my things while you use the bathroom."

"You'd better go first. I'll have to shave."

"It is good of you, Herr Doktor. I shall not trouble to do that now. Perhaps in the morning. I will be quick."

A trivial exchange, but the arrangement was to have enormous consequences for Andrew. If he had taken first use of the bathroom, he would not have observed the peculiar actions of Mr. Kusitch in the bedroom. He would have closed the door on his side and left the little man to himself. But Kusitch, indifferent to matters of privacy—or because of his gregarious need—left the door open on his side when he invited Andrew to take his turn, and then started talking again, asking questions.

"How long have you been away from London?"

"Three years."

"Himmel! I had thought you were tourist. Have you been working to stay so long from your country?"

"That's it."

"In Athens?"

"In Greece. For the International Red Cross."

Lathering his face, Andrew turned towards the doorway. Kusitch was combing his hair. His cheap composition suitcase was open on the bed and he had set out some bottles and tubes on the dressing table.

"Ah! The International Red Cross!" He was having a little difficulty with a bald patch. "The war left much work for you doctors. You found things bad in Greece?"

"Surely, they are bad everywhere in eastern Europe."

"Yes." Kusitch applied some grease to his hair and got to work with a brush. "In my country, too."

"You are not from Greece?"

"Yugoslavia." The little man's tone was suddenly vague as if he had lost interest in the subject. Andrew turned from the doorway and began to use his razor. The bathroom mirror gave him a view of the bedroom, but it missed the section that contained Mr. Kusitch. The questioning voice still came from the position in front of the dressing table.

"Then you go home to London on leave, Herr Doktor?"

Andrew completed a stroke, holding a cheek taut. "No. I've given up the job. I'm going home for good."

"So? You wish no more to be a doctor?"

"I'm taking a hospital post."

He craned forward a little, coming to a place on his upper lip where he had cut himself yesterday. He heard Kusitch padding softly about on the bedroom carpet and caught a glimpse of him in the mirror on a course towards the window. Then, suddenly, he saw a more distant image of Kusitch. He watched because the curious effect interested him. Within the section of the bedroom revealed by the bathroom mirror stood a large antique pier glass. It was slewed round slightly off parallel to the wall and raked forward an inch or two from the vertical, and it was this accidental arrangement that had enlarged his field of vision.

Kusitch, still in his shirtsleeves, was standing on the parquetry beyond the line of the carpet. Andrew went on shaving, but continued to watch the image in the pier glass. Kusitch seemed to be in a dream for a moment. He made a movement behind him, and next he had a manila envelope in his right hand. He crouched down, lifted the carpet, shoved the envelope underneath it, and then pushed an armchair over the spot.

Andrew grinned. The little man wasn't going to risk being waylaid and robbed in this foreign city, so with naïve cunning he left the bulk of his money under the carpet for any dishonest servant to find. But he might be right at that. The obvious hiding places were sometimes the safer. Nevertheless, the precaution was in a way pathetic. What did the little man know of the Herr Doktor he clung to so trustfully? Was honesty so patent in the Maclaren face?

The Herr Doktor cleaned up the Maclaren face with a facecloth and took a look at it in the mirror. He was prejudiced, of course, but it did seem to him that it was fairly engaging as faces went. You would not, perhaps, describe it as particularly handsome, but you could scarcely deny that it was human. Why that girl at the airport should have looked at him as if he were some sort of werewolf he could not imagine.

He turned from the mirror, his spine crawling at the memory of the humiliation. He towelled his face vigorously, angrily. Then, as he looked over the towel's edge directly into the pier glass, he saw something that put the girl from his mind.

Kusitch had just advanced to the bed and picked up his grey tweed jacket, and on the counterpane lay an automatic pistol.

Andrew stared.

There was no mistaking the thing. It showed up clearly, darkly metallic against the pink counterpane.

Kusitch put on the jacket that had covered the weapon. He straightened the lapels and squared his shoulders. He had his back turned towards the bathroom door and, if it had not been for the pier glass, Andrew would never have seen what was on the bed. But Kusitch was as yet unaware of the revealing pier glass. Still with his back to the bathroom, he took up the pistol, held it close to him, opened the magazine, and slid out the clip of cartridges. Then he pressed his thumb into the clip. He was making sure that the slides ran smoothly in the guides. They did. He replaced the clip. Then, as he did so, he looked up and saw the pier glass.

If he was disturbed, he gave no sign of it. He wheeled about and greeted Andrew with a beaming face.

"So," he said. "You feel better that you have shaved, hah?"

"Much better." Andrew tried to make his tone quite casual. "What are you doing with that thing?"

"This!" Kusitch weighed the pistol in his right hand. His eyes probed keenly, but he laughed. "Do not trouble yourself, Herr Doktor. When I travel in strange countries, I like to take my little friend with me. You cannot tell when he will not be of use."

"What are you afraid of?"

Mr. Kusitch shrugged. "It is a precaution." Andrew smiled. "Well, I've been in some tough places, but never one where a pistol would have been much use."

"You are a doctor. My trade is different."

"What is your trade?"

"Do you need to know that, my friend?" Kusitch was gently polishing the grip of his pistol with the ball of his thumb.

"I'm sorry." Andrew spoke a little sharply. "You must forgive me if I seem curious. I was concerned only to know whether you were carrying anything valuable with you."

"Only my life, Herr Doktor."

The shutter flicked behind the grey eyes and Andrew saw mystery again. But it was no longer interesting. Now, it worried him. He had been a fool not to rebuff the man from the start. Almost certainly Kusitch was some sort of criminal. But he had given himself away too soon. If he thought he was going to get anything out of Andrew Maclaren, he was very much mistaken.

Andrew turned abruptly, strode through the bathroom to his own chamber and shut the door firmly. There was no look to the door, and nothing but a bolt on the bathroom side. He seized a shirt and hastily put it on, but before he could fasten the buttons, Kusitch had opened the door and entered.

Andrew turned, his heart throbbing painfully. The little man smiled mournfully and held out empty hands.

"You must not be angry with me, Herr Doktor," he said. "You have cause; I will admit it. I ask questions but do not receive them. I will tell you about my trade, so that you will understand."

"It isn't at all necessary." Andrew fumbled with the buttons of his shirt. He felt foolish now. He scowled.

"Pardon, but I think so," Kusitch said with dignity. "There must be no suspicion between us."

"Suspicion?"

"In your mind, Herr Doktor. You think perhaps that I am a thief who makes friendly to steal from you. Do not deny, Herr Doktor. Perhaps, even an assassin!" Kusitch lifted his arms from his sides and let them fall helplessly. "I am none of these things. I am a policeman, an investigator. It is inevitable in my trade that I make enemies, but these enemies are the criminals, the thieves, the assassins. I am a peaceful man. I like nothing better than to be with my wife and child in Dubrovnik, but my superiors order otherwise. I think sometimes they inflate their ideas of my talents, but. . . so!" Again the gesture with the arms. "They send me abroad on missions. They train me to see that my pistol is properly loaded; to have it ready for my need."

His right hand flashed up and across his chest and under his jacket in a practised movement. The pistol was there, in a sling under his left arm, but he left it there. The movement was merely a gesture.

Andrew examined him with new interest. The look in the grey eyes; the quick, searching, almost furtive glances. A man seeking, or a man with the fear of being sought. A policeman. Of course.

Suddenly, Andrew's sense of humour returned. He laughed.

Kusitch pursed his lips.

"You must understand of course that I am not an ordinary policeman," he said. "My work is a speciality. I find stolen property. The thieves are no concern of mine, except if they lead me to the property."

"What sort of property?" Andrew asked.

"The national treasures of my country." Mr. Kusitch could not resist a small attitude. "The treasures looted by Hitler's agents and others during the late war. You see, Herr Doktor, before the Germans arrived I was an art dealer. My establishment in Belgrade was an international centre. In particular I was fortunate with Slavonic art. I had connections with many capitals: Paris, London,

Rome, New York. I travelled. I knew many lands. In the war I lost everything. After the liberation, the state had need of my services and I gave them. You will appreciate that I am equipped for my new trade. I am an expert. I know the things I seek. I have some languages. Perhaps I make faults in my English, but German is like my native tongue. My French passes; my Italian is fair. My colleagues tell me I am poor in psychology, yet I succeed in my trade. Already I have recovered many treasures from Germany and Austria. The English and the American occupation authorities have been very kind, very helpful; especially in Germany."

"And now you're on the way to England? Do you mean to tell me you hope to find some of the loot there?"

"It has been dispersed. The paintings, the statues, the objets d'art, the precious books have been scattered wide and far."

"What are you looking for this time? Paintings? Books?"

"Ah, please, Herr Doktor. You will permit me to be discreet. Also, it is getting late. I think we should go to our dinner. Yes?"

"Yes."

Mr. Kusitch was the complete guide. He did everything. Andrew had not even to lift a finger to the row of buttons in the clanging, shuddering lift. Kusitch negotiated the exchange of traveller's cheques at the *caisse*, hailed the taxi drivers, gave the directions, and after it was all over Andrew had little knowledge of where he had been. He retained only the impressions of places visited. The one name he caught was the Rue des Croisades. The restaurant was in a street off or somewhere beyond the Rue des Croisades.

It was a small restaurant. You went through a partitioned shop front affair with a cash desk and a pastry counter, and entered a long, narrow room with banquettes upholstered in a faded red material. There were two rows of tables separated by a central aisle, and at the far end a large mirror that made the room seem twice as long. Andrew remembered little more than this about it except that the food was good.

There were not many diners. Kusitch demanded a table at the far end, and shepherded his companion forward. The waiter drew the table out a little to make the banquette accessible, and Andrew moved to take the seat. Kusitch intervened.

"If you do not mind, I prefer the banquette," he said. "I am always in danger from draughts. Even very small draughts. It is my lumbago."

So Kusitch sat with his back to the wall, and his sharp eyes searched the room, inspecting the patrons, examining every new arrival, and once again, in an unguarded moment, there was a mystery in his eyes that might have been fear.

He talked. He professed to like his new trade. It gave him freedom. It enabled him to travel. Much as he loved Yugoslavia, much as he approved the policies of Tito, he was essentially a man of the world. Rome, New York, Paris. If only he had an art shop in Paris, he would never go back to Yugoslavia.

"Why go back anyway?" Andrew demanded. "You have knowledge. You say you are an expert. Aren't there any of your old friends who would help you?"

"Haven't I told you that I have a wife and child in Dubrovnik?"

"You mean that they . . . ?"

"Are in Dubrovnik, Herr Doktor," Kusitch interrupted firmly. "It is all quite simple. I think we should have another bottle of wine."

For a moment or two, Andrew's mind toyed with the possibility that perhaps "it" was all not merely quite simple but a trifle over simple. Then he put this unworthy thought away. In any case, simple or complex, "it" was none of his business. He got on with his dinner.

They had the second bottle of wine, and Kusitch called for the bill. Andrew insisted on paying his share, and Kusitch yielded. They went on to a crowded and noisy café for coffee and cognac. Kusitch concentrated on the cognac, and, after several glasses of it, began to grow a little thick in speech, heavy of eye, and sombre in mood. He talked of painting: of Picasso and Matisse and Dufy and Rouault, but what he said of them meant little to Andrew. He had the impression that Kusitch himself was only half aware of its meaning and that there were other anxieties on the little man's mind.

It was nearly midnight when they returned to the Risler-Moircy, and Kusitch was almost asleep on his feet. Andrew tried the hot water and took a bath. By the time he had dried himself, Kusitch was snoring. When he slid back the bolt on Kusitch's side, he pulled the door open and glanced in; wondering if the other had undressed. He had. The little man was lying on his back, tucked up to the chin. The pistol on the bedside table glinted dully in the light that spilled out from the bathroom. Andrew closed the door silently, repeated the action on his own side, and went to his divan.

He had been very tired, but the bath had freshened him up. He tried to read a pocket edition of a spy story, but his mind would not stay on the printed page. The gunplay of fictional characters in a battle over secret papers was poor stuff compared to that unfired pistol in the next room, and every reference to papers reminded him of the packet that Kusitch had slipped under the carpet. Half dozing, he fitted the packet into a fantasy of his own, and somehow the girl in the plane came into it. Her objective was that packet under the carpet. She had followed the desperate Kusitch across Europe, and it was possible that she was now in this hotel, awaiting her opportunity to act. Naturally she had scorned the approach of the handsome young doctor. Duty must come before pleasure. As soon as Kusitch was asleep . . .

The snoring of Kusitch sounded through the wall and the two closed doors of the bathroom. It went on monotonously, loudly. Then, suddenly, after a long gurgling that ended in a gasp, it stopped. Kusitch must have turned on his side.

In the new silence the lift whined and clanged. Next there was a creaking from the window. Andrew rose wearily and padded across the carpet. A breeze was getting up outside, and the French window swung on its hinges. He had opened it earlier on, ignoring a request from Kusitch to keep it shut. Now he fastened it and went back to bed.

Kusitch began to snore again.

Andrew read, yawned, thought of that impossible girl, read again, dozed, roused himself to reach for the switch at his bedside, then dropped down into darkness.

When he came back to consciousness with a start, it seemed that he had slept for a long time. It might have been an hour, or two hours, but he never knew.

Even in the moment of waking he was sure that a sound from the next room had disturbed him. He described it to himself as a stifled shout, a cry from Kusitch in his sleep. It could have been something in a dream, but it had seemed very real, and he sat up, listening intently in the silence.

Then he remembered the little man's warning about his restlessness, his fear of falling out of bed. Perhaps he really did fall out of bed.

At last he heard confirmatory sounds: the creaking of bedsprings, a shuffling, a muffled imprecation as if Kusitch had got his head tangled up in the bedclothes. That was it. Kusitch was struggling to free himself. The springs complained again as he tossed about, but were quickly relieved of his weight. The struggle ended in a thud. A weighty thud. The double bed had not saved Kusitch. He had fallen out of it.

Andrew laughed silently. It was callous. The poor fellow could have hurt himself. On the other hand, he could always call for help if he needed it.

Andrew waited. There was no call for help. He heard a grunting forced by a laboured effort. There was more shuffling. The springs creaked, and it seemed obvious to Andrew that Kusitch had crawled into bed again. He lay back on his divan and pulled up the bedclothes, hoping he would get to sleep before the snoring was renewed.

He did. He slept undisturbed until eight o'clock. The day was sunny, the room bright with morning light. He sprang from his bed, unfastened the window and did his breathing exercises.

Next he tried the bathroom door but found that it was bolted against him.

He called, grinning to himself. "You in there, Kusitch? How did you sleep?"

No answer. He waited. There were none of the familiar sounds from the bathroom; only silence.

Andrew snorted irritably. This was what happened when you had communicating doors. This was the result of sharing a suite with a careless foreigner.

He knocked loudly and shouted. "Hi! Kusitch! If you're not using the bathroom, unbolt the door!"

He knocked more loudly, waited, shouted again.

Damn the man!

He put his raincoat over his pyjamas and padded out into the corridor. He hammered on the bedroom door, but no answer came from within. He grasped the doorknob, intent on making it rattle. He turned the knob, and the door opened.

The room was empty. Kusitch's underclothes had gone. So had his hat, his coat and his composition suitcase. Except for the tumbled bed and the bedclothes trailing on the floor there was nothing to show that the room had even been occupied.

Three

ANDREW'S FIRST THOUGHT naturally was that the man had dressed and gone downstairs to wait for him. It was not, perhaps, an action in the character of the clinging Yugoslav, but you might as well believe in Santa Claus as look for consistency in human beings. Scots excepted of course. Andrew shrugged it off, went to the bathroom, slipped back the bolt and followed his morning routine.

It was not until he was putting away his toilet things that a new thought about Kusitch came to him. The man hadn't used the bathroom that morning. The articles he had deposited untidily on shelf and washbasin were just as he had left them overnight: the tube of toothpaste uncapped, the toothbrush lying across the aluminium soap container, the shaving brush held to the razor case by a wide rubber band. The soap was dry; the shaving brush, too. He had said that he was going to shave in the morning.

Perhaps he had gone down to the street to find a barber? Then why had he taken his valise with him? And, if he had packed up to continue his journey to London, why had he left these things in the bathroom? All his other possessions were gone, including the various bottles of pills and lotions from the dressing table. Where the pistol had rested on the bedside table, the key of the room now lay. Kusitch had finished with it.

Andrew picked it up and locked the door, returned through the bathroom to his own chamber, dressed hastily, took the key down to the desk and made inquiries about Kusitch. The reception clerk had not seen him. The porter shook his head and suggested that he might have gone in to breakfast.

Andrew went in to breakfast. There were only a few persons in the restaurant and Kusitch was not among them. Andrew sat facing the entrance, watching every arrival. He ate a brioche and drank his coffee. There was not much time left then.

He hurried back upstairs, hoping that Kusitch had returned, that he might even be waiting in the corridor outside the locked doors.

The corridor was empty; the doors were still locked.

Andrew threw the forgotten possessions of Kusitch into his own bag, descended to the foyer again, ordered a taxi, surrendered his key and asked for his bill. While he waited, he watched the entrance door. The lift came shuddering down and stopped with a crash. He turned in the direction of the machine as a solitary passenger issued from the cage, carrying a light valise. It was not Kusitch. It was the girl with red hair, the girl addressed as Miss Meriden by the air hostess of the plane from Athens.

Possibly it was the surprise of seeing her here that made him start, yet there could be nothing logically surprising in the fact that she, too, had stayed at the Risler-Moircy. He had, indeed, allotted her a room here in his little fiction of the night.

She stared straight at his left ear as she came towards the desk, but gave no sign that she had ever seen him before or that she was seeing anything of him but his ear now. She looked almost aggressively healthy and self-sufficient. "Smug" was the word that came to Andrew's mind. A clerk appeared to attend to her as if he had been waiting all his life for this opportunity.

"My bill, please!" she demanded, and one felt that the Queen of Sheba would have been less imperious. "Miss Ruth Meriden. And I have to catch the ten o'clock plane. Will you get me a taxi right away, please?"

"Certainly, mademoiselle." He snapped his fingers and a porter came running.

Here was a chance for a good deed that a Boy Scout would have jumped at. "If you don't mind sharing, I have a taxi already waiting to take me to the air terminal." With a slight bow, of course.

Andrew kept his lips together grimly. He watched the girl in the mirror behind the counter. She might be tiresome, but she was undeniably beautiful. She turned her head and for an instant, through the mirror, their eyes met. At that moment his bill arrived.

He looked at the amount, and it was more than he had expected. It gave him a scare. He wondered if he had enough money left to meet it. He had not budgeted for any possible delays, and, after his expenditure on dinner with Kusitch, he was down to a few franc notes and his last traveller's cheque. After the first scare came something like panic. He thought of asking the clerk if he could take a cheque on his London bank. He was pulled up by the further thought that this would be a contravention of the currency regulations. He looked at the bill again, almost incredulously; and then he understood what had happened.

"This is made out for the suite," he said. "I just want the bill for my room. I have nothing to do with Mr. Kusitch. He will pay for his own room."

"I'm sorry, sir! It is not the practice to separate the rooms in the accounting. The suite was engaged in the names of yourself and your friend."

"Very well. I'll pay half. You can collect the rest from Kusitch."

"Pardon, sir. Your friend seems to have gone on ahead of you. You yourself handed in his key. We assume, of course, that you will make yourself responsible for the full amount."

"I'm not responsible for Mr. Kusitch in any way."

"But you occupied the suite, sir. The amount is not much more than our usual tariff for room and bath."

"No doubt it's reasonable, but I don't know how much money I've got left."

It was ridiculous. The girl at the counter was listening, taking in the whole farcical scene, no doubt with a smirk of amusement on her smug face. He did not dare to look into the mirror. He knew his face was getting redder, and part of the hot blood was a rising indignation at the behaviour of Kusitch. It was clear enough now why Kusitch had skipped, but he wasn't going to get away with it, by heaven! The amount of the whole bill might be insignificant, but he'd exact the full half of it from Kusitch. Policeman, was he? Well, we'd soon see about that!

He was turning out his pockets like a boy in a sweet shop, putting the money on the desk in front of him—francs, some paper drachmas, his lucky penny. The whole lot didn't amount to a half of what was needed.

By now the other clerk was there with Miss Meriden's bill, and she, too, was putting money on the counter; but from a well-stocked wallet. He was within the range of a delicate perfume that probably came from something in her open handbag, a perfume that would have cost her more per ounce than the whole amount of this wretched hotel bill.

He surveyed his collection of currency and pulled out his pocketbook, and then, as he opened the worn pigskin, he sighed with relief. Instead of one, he had two traveller's cheques left, and they were plenty. He signed them, and the polite clerk took them to the *caisse*.

The girl was still at the counter. He kept his eyes lowered. He caught a glimpse of her hands moving beside him, reaching for her receipt, tucking it away, closing her bag. And her hands were something of a shock to him. They were fine hands, strong and capable, but they suggested a worker rather than one who lived in decorative idleness. They were cared for, obviously, but were marked by cuts and scars. The right thumb wore an adhesive bandage. The left forefinger had a blue bruise under a broken nail, as if it had received a whack with a hammer.

He had, perhaps, two seconds to notice these curious details. Then the hands were withdrawn, and he was aware that she had left the counter. He looked up and saw her back, a receding image in the mirror, followed by the porter with her valise. A mirror on the opposite side of the foyer returned a reflection of her approach, and he saw her serene face again with its corona of red-gold hair. He continued to stare after she had gone, seeing himself reflected back and forth. The place had more mirrors in it than the Palace of Versailles. Someone must have had a mania for . . .

He remembered suddenly the doubly-reflected picture of Kusitch stooping in the corner of his room, shoving the manila envelope under the carpet. He hoped Kusitch hadn't forgotten that envelope, because it probably contained his money and the man was going to need it to pay his share of the confounded bill.

"Your taxi, monsieur."

He followed the porter. He saw Ruth Meriden again as her cab drove away from the hotel, and in another moment his own cab started as if in pursuit.

There was quite a crowd at the terminal building. He checked the number of his plane and found the official who was dealing with the passengers. Flight 263—that was the designation. The girl was the fourth person ahead of him, and there was still no sign of Kusitch.

Andrew was still the last in the line when he reached the desk. He asked about Kusitch.

"Kusitch?" The official looked at his passenger list. "I've no one of that name."

"But you must have," Andrew protested. "It's the ten o'clock plane to London, isn't it?"

"Certainly, sir. Flight two-six-three."

"Then Mr. Kusitch is a passenger. We travelled together from Athens yesterday. We reserved seats for this morning as soon as we heard the night plane for London was grounded. Kusitch *must* be on your list. He has the seat next to mine."

Andrew became vehement. The official shook his head, then hesitated.

"Perhaps there has been a cancellation," he suggested. "Just a moment. I'll find out."

He picked up a telephone, pressed a button, and made his inquiry. He spoke to Andrew, holding a hand over the receiver." That's right, sir . . . P. G. Kusitch. He cancelled his reservation. The seat has been given to Major Bardolph."

Andrew felt anger rising. What sort of damn-fool game was the fellow playing? Skipping out of the hotel with his bill unpaid, leaving his things in the bathroom.

"When did the man cancel his seat?"

The official passed on the question and transmitted the answer to Andrew.

"Last night, sir. He telephoned."

"But that's impossible. I'm sure he never left his room. He was in bed, asleep."

"Nevertheless . . ."

Andrew began to feel a little sick. He pressed a hand on the desk before him. "Please," he said. "Can you find out the time your people got the message?"

The official put through the additional inquiry. There was a short wait. Then he announced: "Our record says twenty-two thirty-three hours. Monsieur Kusitch telephoned in person."

"Ten-thirty!" Andrew shivered as if a blast of cold air had touched him. "At ten-thirty I was with Mr. Kusitch in a café, drinking coffee and cognac. He definitely did not telephone."

"But surely, sir? He has not come to claim his seat. That proves that he must have cancelled it."

Andrew gazed at the man incredulously. He had a queer feeling in his stomach and icy fingers seemed to be pressing him in the small of the back. He put both hands on the desk and leaned heavily.

"I was with Kusitch all the evening," he asserted. "From seven o'clock on he was scarcely out of my sight. We left the hotel together and did not get back till after midnight. Kusitch never went near a telephone in that time."

"Possibly he had someone pass on the message for him?"

"No. He never had the slightest intention of giving up his seat in the plane. He was anxious to get to London as soon as possible."

"Then where is he, sir?" "I don't know. The last I saw of him, he was in bed . . ."

He broke off, suddenly recalling the sounds in the night. He had interpreted them so amusingly. He had imagined the comical figure of Mr. Kusitch falling out of bed and climbing back again. That was a laugh, a good laugh. He heard the bedsprings creaking. Again he felt the cold touch at the bottom of the spine. He had known fear more than once in his life, but this was a different kind of fear. He pulled himself together, shaking away the sickness, and in the instant he knew what he had to do.

"There's something wrong," he told the official. "You'd better make full inquiries about that phone call. I'm going back to the hotel. Can you switch my seat to the afternoon plane?"

"But, Dr. Maclaren, the bus is about to leave for the airport."

"This is serious. It may be very serious indeed. If you can't put somebody else in my seat, I'll have to pay an extra fare."

"Some people are waiting, but at this late hour it is very difficult."

"Can you get me on an afternoon plane?"

"There's a vacancy on Flight seven-four-nine, two-thirty."

"All right. Find out about that telephone call. The police may want to know."

Andrew checked his bag at the luggage office and strode off quickly. Outside he passed the bus loaded with the passengers for Flight 263. It was waiting; waiting for him. The red-haired girl sat well up towards the front, and now the customary serenity of her face was marred by a slight frown of impatience. For a moment he regretted that he had given up his seat. That was curious; but, of course, it was simply that he realised that he was meddling with something that did not concern him. What was Kusitch to him that he should put himself to any trouble over the man?

He halted. All the doubts he had entertained about Kusitch went through his mind again. The man's story might have been wholly false. He could be something silly like a spy. He could have chosen to disappear in the middle of the night, suddenly apprehensive of one of those enemies he had talked about. He could be a criminal with quite another motive for performing a vanishing trick. And he could be merely an unhappy creature with persecution fantasies, a paranoiac.

All the probable and improbable explanations wheeled in Andrew's head, but none of them altered the basic situation. Kusitch had dropped out of sight, and he, Andrew Maclaren, was the one man who could do something about it. If he did nothing, if he washed his hands of the whole affair and went on to London, no one might ever hear another word of Kusitch.

How it had happened he could not say, but Kusitch seemed to have established a claim on him. He had wanted to get rid of the little man. He had found him a bore and a nuisance; but he had also found him pathetic. Andrew could see again the hurt-dog look of appeal in the round face, and it was an appeal he could not resist. It might have been instinct, a hunch, an extrasensory perception of some other kind, but he believed in that instant that Kusitch was in danger of his life, and that he had to do something about it.

He hurried past the bus and hailed the first taxi he saw. In seven minutes he was back at the Risler-Moircy. He would not have been surprised to find police cars drawn up in front of the entrance and the foyer swarming with plain-clothes men and uniformed agents. There was nothing, not even a porter in the foyer. A young couple emerged from the restaurant deep in an argument. That was all. It was the midmorning lull when the Risler-Moircy relaxed and yawned. The clerk at the reception counter seemed half asleep.

Andrew explained that he had left something in his room. The clerk, completely indifferent, produced the key at once. People were always leaving things in their rooms it seemed: pocketbooks, trinkets, dead bodies.

The idea came to Andrew with horrifying impact. He hadn't thought of that before, but now the one thing in his mind was the door of the clothes cupboard in the double bedroom.

The lift was shuddering about somewhere near the top of the building. Andrew could not wait for it. He ran up the stairs and was breathing heavily when he reached the third floor. The door of the sitting room was open. He paused a moment, then walked in, surprising one of the floor maids who was stripping the divan.

She was full of apologies. She thought Monsieur had departed. If she was in the way, she would return later.

He told her to carry on, and repeated the excuse he had made to the clerk.

The girl hesitated, gathering up the used linen in her arms. He asked her if she had done the other room, and she replied that she had. She had not noticed any forgotten property.

"I'll look," he told her, and all the while he was trying to hide the fact that his nerves were jumping.

He closed and bolted the bathroom door so that she could not follow him. Once he was in the room he had no hesitation. He went to the clothes cupboard and pulled the door open. There was nothing there. Not even a coat hanger on the rail, let alone a corpse.

There was sweat on him. He could feel the prickle of it and was annoyed. He had seen enough of death, God knows, and he should, as a professional man, have been able to face a corpse unemotionally. Yet this time the thought of it had come too close to him. He stood staring into the empty cupboard, quite still for a moment. The reprieve was for him and not for Kusitch, yet it made him believe that Kusitch was still alive, however illogical this new belief might be.

He shut the cupboard door and looked round the room. He went to the corner near the window and lifted the carpet with his toe.

The manila envelope was still there.

To his mind it was positive proof that Kusitch had not left the hotel voluntarily. If he had done so, he must surely have taken the envelope with him. The suggestion had been that he had hidden it because it contained money or a means of drawing money. In that case he would not have departed without it.

Andrew stooped, holding the carpet back. The envelope lay flap down and there was nothing written on the exposed side. He hesitated. The correct thing was to leave it as it was and notify the police; touch nothing. But he had to know what was in the envelope; besides, it might not be safe to leave it under the carpet.

He picked up the packet and allowed the carpet to fall back into place. As he straightened himself, he heard someone trying the bathroom door, turning the handle. The door creaked as pressure was applied to it, and a male voice asked in French if anyone was there. The voice had an accent that Andrew could not identify. It was provincial, perhaps: Walloon, Flemish, or whatever they called it. Another servant, he thought, and resented the peremptory note in the voice. Let him wait.

Andrew was at the window, peering at the package as if, by concentration, his eyes might see through the opaque manila paper that kept its secret. The envelope measured about seven and a half by five inches. The contents made a mass whose area might have been covered by a pound note. The mass was not very thick, but such a tightly packed wad, if it were indeed composed of pound notes, must have represented a substantial sum of money; something like two hundred or so. Tentatively, he pushed a finger beneath the flap of the envelope. He could feel that the flap was only lightly gummed. He slid his finger forward. The flap sprang. The envelope was open.

The wad was a booklet. Andrew took it out, stared at the green paper binding, blinked at it, and stared again. At first sight it was just unbelievable, but no amount of gazing at it would effect a transformation. The legend upon it was fixed in white lettering: "A London Transport Publication." And then, following the symbol of circle and bisecting bar: GREEN LINE COACH GUIDE.

Andrew thumbed hastily through the stapled pages of timetables, but saw nothing between die leaves; not a solitary bank note, not even a key to the cipher of the Yugoslav secret police.

It was anticlimax, and the sudden release of tension made him feel curiously weary. He dropped the envelope on the floor and put the Green Line Coach Guide in his pocket. Then he sat down in the window and looked across the room at the newly made bed. He smiled ruefully, thinking of Kusitch. Bits of behaviour, remembered fragments of speech, now came together to form a pattern. The pistol, the manila envelope, locked doors, fastened windows, wall-backed seats, searching looks, confidences, the pathetic clinging to the chance company of a fellow passenger . . . The man must live in a most extraordinary world of fantasy; a world in which a Green Line Coach Guide became the plans of the Petropavlovsky Fort or the blueprints of a hydrogen bomb, a nightmare world in which there were enemies behind every pillar. The man's conscious mind, of course, had really nothing to do with it. He was dominated by his fantasies and they followed a classic pattern. He was the sufferer, the persecuted. Not all his persecutors were projected, of course. Some stayed inside: epilepsy, lumbago, the liver complaint. And the hostages in Dubrovnik, the imaginary wife and child. Heaven alone knew what new terror had seized him in the night after his fall from the bed. By now he might be on his way to Warsaw or Waziristan. There was still that phone call to the air terminal to be considered, but no doubt there was a simple explanation.

Andrew felt himself cheated. He felt doubly cheated when he thought of the plane that would be taking off for London in a very few minutes. And somehow Miss Ruth Meriden, her red hair, cool eyes, smug look and all, got mixed up with his regrets. It was curious that he should have a feeling of emptiness when he considered that it was unlikely he would ever see her again; curious, because he despised the type and found the individual wholly objectionable. It was even more curious that he should now begin to blame Kusitch bitterly for the sense of loss that came over him.

There was nothing more to do in the hotel. He went into the bathroom, threw back the bolt in the farther door, and entered the living room. A man rose from an armchair and wheeled to face him.

"Pardon for my disturbance," he said. "I wish to see the suite by the permission of the chambermaid. My room has not the comfort. I make change-over when you are departing."

The voice was that of the man who had tried the bathroom door. His English was worse than his French, but more revealing. The accent was German. So was the parade-ground arrogance. His tone was sharp and accusing. He said, in effect: "Why are you holding me up? Get the hell out of it, and be quick!"

At that moment Andrew was not in a conciliatory frame of mind. "Where I come from," he said, "it's customary to wait till a room is vacated before moving in."

"I have no need for instruction. I make no fault. The chambermaid tells me the Englishman is departing."

"I haven't departed yet. And I'm not English."

"No? This is not the right suite, perhaps? The maid said the Englishman and a friend were to leave this morning."

The man was tall and lean. He had a nose that looked as if it had been stropped to a fine edge. His mouth was a hard line between thin and shapeless lips. The eyes were black, and quick with animal menace, but the rest of the face had the wooden immobility of a ventriloquist's dummy. The lower jaw moved when required; only the eyes were alive. They narrowed aggressively, demanding an answer from Andrew. When they failed to get it, the mouth moved again.

"Perhaps your friend is in the next room? The maid makes more mistakes?"

The maid returned along the corridor and hesitated in the open doorway. She saw that the situation was unfortunate, and turned a worried look on Andrew.

"Pardon, monsieur. I am sorry you have been disturbed." Then she spoke in German to the tall man. "I asked you to wait till the suite was ready, Herr Schlegel."

The reply came quickly and harshly. "You told me the suite was empty. You are a fool. Get out of my way."

He walked with a stiff gait that might have been due to a mechanical limb. He thrust out a hand to wave the girl aside. Andrew stopped him.

"Now that you're here, you can look the place over," he said. "I'm going. I've finished." "Did you find what you wanted, monsieur?" the girl asked him.

"Yes. I found it, thanks. Good-bye."

He looked back from the first turn in the corridor. Herr Schlegel was standing in the doorway of the sitting room, watching him.

Four

HE COUNTED his francs. He had enough for lunch, a taxi fare, and all foreseeable incidentals. Down in the foyer again, he consulted a plan of the city and decided to take a walk. He had time to kill and he did not know Brussels. He took his bearings from the position of the Risler-Moircy and mapped a short tour.

The morning was sunny, the air mild, and there were interesting things to observe in the unfamiliar streets. He found the Grande Place and inspected the Hôtel de Ville and the Maison du Roi. He was just beginning to enjoy himself when something odd happened.

He had the impression that he was being followed.

It was absurd, of course; a hangover from Mr. Kusitch! Yet he could not quite dispel the impression. There was a man who loitered at one corner of the Maison du Roi when he stepped out into the square to get a perspective view of the façade. He was sure he had seen the same man a few minutes earlier in the Place de Brouckère. But was there anything strange in that? Any citizen in good standing was at liberty to take a stroll along the Boulevard Anspach and around to the Grande Place on a sunny morning. Or at any time and in any weather for that matter.

Andrew blamed himself for a fool. It was time he relaxed and forgot Kusitch, or before you could say "dementia praecox" he'd have the disagreeable Herr Schlegel waiting for him in a dark alley. Why on earth should anyone follow him, unless it was to get him alone on some quiet corner and try to sell him a set of art postcards?

He made his way back to the Rue de la Madeleine. So did the man. He turned to the left, walked a few yards, wheeled about and proceeded in the direction of the Place Royale. So did the man. He was a thickset fellow in a drab green raincoat with part of a plump florid face visible below the wide brim of a green soft hat.

It was no longer easy to laugh off the thing as mere coincidence. Andrew made further tests. Whenever he stopped to look in a shop window, the green soft hat also became interested in a shop window. The fellow was a fool at the game, or he did not care if he was observed. The one certain thing about him was his persistence.

Andrew was no longer intrigued by the sights of Brussels. Turning from the Place Royale into the street of the same name, he was refitting his former fears to the case of Mr. Kusitch and seeking new explanations for the things he had dismissed as the fantasies of a psychotic. Even the Green Line Coach Guide could be explained if you exercised a little ingenuity.

Once more Andrew saw Kusitch as the victim, a man who had been snatched away in the night. Instead of dawdling round Brussels, he should have gone to the police, should have seen at once that the Coach Guide was a blind, a nose-to-thumb gesture.

He looked back and saw the green soft hat about twenty yards away, and now he had the taste of fear in his own mouth. That shadow was the agent of those who had kidnapped Kusitch. It was a sinister shadow, full of evil.

Andrew turned the corner of the Rue de la Loi. He saw a taxi, called to the driver, and ran for it. He was in the cab before it could come to a standstill and at once he urged the driver to accelerate. Instead the man stopped and turned to glare doubtfully at his fare.

"Where do you wish to go?" he asked.

"*Commissariat de Police. Vite!*"

The driver was surprised. His look said plainly that he had been entirely mistaken. He muttered something that might have been an apology. The cab shot forward, but the moment of advantage had been lost. The green soft hat was stepping into another taxi, and the chase was still on.

At the Commissariat everybody was very calm and polite. They were obviously quite accustomed to visits from foreigners who wished to report suspected cases of kidnapping, or perhaps they did not quite understand Andrew's French. He had to wait for a while. Then a detective who could speak English came along. By this time Andrew's fears had grown and to his explanation he added his belief that Kusitch might have been murdered. The English-speaking detective appeared to be impressed. There was another slight delay, and then Andrew was taken along a corridor to meet Inspector Jordaens.

A dry, impassive man, Inspector Jordaens, with dry, impassive English.

"Dr. Maclaren," he said, "we have checked with the airport officials concerning this man Kusitch. Pyotr Grigorievitch Kusitch, a servant of the Yugoslav Government in transit to London. His passport was quite in order. Can you tell me why he elected to travel from Dubrovnik via Athens?"

"I can't," Andrew answered. "I did think it peculiar."

"Why?"

"For the same reason that you do, I suppose. I would have been inclined to take a shorter route."

"Exactly. Unless, perhaps, you wished to see the Acropolis?"

"What has that to do with it?"

"Exactly. Dr. Maclaren, I will listen to your story. Be brief, if you please. Just give me the facts."

Andrew was brief. A stenographer took notes. On the whole, Inspector Jordaens was a good listener, but occasionally he would interrupt with comments or questions that had a disturbing effect upon Andrew.

"So you stayed at the Risler-Moircy? You are aware, of course, that it is a hotel of unimpeachable reputation?"

And: "Do you really suggest that kidnappers could enter such a place and remove a guest during the night?" After each sentence he pursed his lips.

When he came to a general examination of Andrew's statement his tone expressed open incredulity. He suggested that Kusitch had voluntarily left the hotel; that the decision might have come as a result of the man's talk about his former business as an art dealer. Kusitch was, on Dr. Maclaren's own evidence, a whimsical fellow, a little curious, perhaps, and, being stimulated by cognac, an impulse had come to him, an irresistible impulse. The grounding of the London plane was an opportunity out of the sky. He would disappear in Brussels. He would abandon his mission, desert, and no one in Yugoslavia would ever hear of him again, not even his wife and child. The alternative was to suppose that the man was mad, quite irresponsible.

Andrew said: "You do not explain the telephone call cancelling his seat on the ten o'clock plane. That call did not come from Kusitch."

"You are very positive, Dr. Maclaren." Inspector Jordaens smiled tolerantly. "I have had a lifetime of experience with witnesses, and I have frequently observed that when they are most positive it is then that they are deceiving themselves." He held up a hand to arrest an interruption. "Wait a moment! I am not referring solely to you. I have first in mind the telephonist at the air terminal who took the message. You were informed that it came in at twenty-two hours thirty-three, but let us suppose that there was a mistake in the recording, that it actually came in at two hours thirty-three. Remember, it was the day telephonist from whom the information came. He may have misread the record."

"You could check that up with the man who was on night duty."

"Assuredly. I am merely putting to you the hypothesis of error. When I come to your evidence, I must raise another question. You say you were with Kusitch from the time you left the hotel until you returned?"

"Yes."

"You dined and drank wine, you went to a café and drank coffee and cognac. You were in this cafe at twenty-two hours thirty-three?"

"Positively."

"And do you still say positively that Kusitch was never out of your sight?"

"Why? What do you mean?"

"I mean, Dr. Maclaren, that when we are called on to give evidence, the commonplace acts, the routine calls, like the postman in the story by your Chesterton, escape our notice. The most familiar things are the most easily forgotten. Do you agree?"

"But this is not merely an academic question, Inspector."

"It is not." Jordaens' dry voice crackled like brown paper. "I put it to you, Dr. Maclaren, that at some time or other during the evening you or Kusitch might possibly have gone to the lavabos alone."

It was true. Andrew was shaken as his strong point collapsed. He might argue that there was nothing to prove that Kusitch had telephoned the cancellation message; he had to admit now that the little man might have done so.

"If you like," the Inspector said dryly, "we will go to the café and examine the proximity of the telephone to the toilet."

Andrew frowned. "I don't know where the place is. I never even noticed the name. I left everything to Kusitch."

"That is unfortunate, Dr. Maclaren."

By implication it was more deplorably unfortunate that an idiotic foreigner should trouble the police with his nonsensical fears. Andrew saw that no words would convince the Inspector that Kusitch might have been kidnapped or murdered. So far he had hesitated about mentioning the Green Line Coach Guide, and now he believed that it would be unwise to do so. His own immediate reaction to that discovery had been to diagnose Kusitch as a pathological case, and the Inspector would seize on that point immediately, since it supported so strongly his own argument. Already, Andrew feared, he was himself being considered from a pathological standpoint.

"No, Dr. Maclaren," Jordaens said, "I believe you are putting too strong an interpretation upon these little incidents of the night. Your anxiety for this chance acquaintance is highly creditable, but I am afraid I do not share it with you. You are a scientific man. You will acknowledge readily that we have to temper imagination with caution."

This was a little too much. Andrew flushed. "How do you temper the fact that I've been shadowed all round Brussels this morning?"

For the first time Inspector Jordaens smiled, a wry, sardonic sort of smile.

"You are positive, Dr. Maclaren?"

The word "positive" had become a term of derision. Andrew's annoyance increased. "You can assure yourself of that," he snapped. "I've already told you he followed me here. No doubt he's waiting for me outside your front door."

"Yes? In a green hat, I think you said." The Inspector's smile became almost infectious, but Andrew was immune to it. "Have no fear," Jordaens went on. "We shall see that no harm comes to you. When you leave here, a detective will be behind you. I suggest that you go straight to the air terminal. Here." He indicated the route on a street plan. "My man will report to you when you reach the terminal building. If you are followed, he will continue to guard you till your bus leaves for the airport."

"What are you going to do about Kusitch? Nothing?"

"On the contrary, Doctor, everything. He may be in danger as you sincerely believe. In any case, we are not disposed to neglect these refugees from the Communist countries until we are sure of their good faith. In this sense we are indebted to you for your promptness in reporting the disappearance."

Andrew's sigh was of heartfelt relief; he had a better opinion of the Inspector, but he tucked the Coach Guide lower in his pocket. He asked: "What am I to do with Kusitch's razor and the other things I took from the bathroom? They're in my bag at the terminal building."

"Hand them to the detective. We shall take care of them." The Inspector rose from his chair. "We have your description of Kusitch. If we can find him, he shall be found."

"I've given you my London address. I would like to know what happens."

The Inspector's smile became amiable. "I will write to you myself. Adieu, Dr. Maclaren. Thank you for coming in. Perhaps your Yugoslav friend will be at the terminal, waiting for the next plane to London."

But he wasn't. Andrew waited just inside the main hall, and, in less than a minute, the promised detective addressed him. Monsieur would be happy to know that he had not been followed from headquarters by any stranger.

It was no news to him. He had looked for the green soft hat and failed to see it The hat had been scared off by the fact that he had gone to the police. But Inspector Jordaens would not look at it in that way. Inspector Jordaens would produce one of his sardonic smiles, or perhaps merely grunt.

Andrew retrieved his bag from the luggage office and handed over Kusitch's property. The detective gave him an itemised receipt: one shaving brush, one safety razor in case with three blades, et cetera. On leaving, he expressed confidence that Monsieur would have no further trouble from men in green hats, and this time the police prophecy was justified. Andrew did not go far from the terminal building for his lunch. He returned from the restaurant just in time to check in and board his bus with the other passengers; but he did not relax until the plane was in the air.

Then he lay back in his seat and closed his eyes. He dozed, he shifted, he felt something pressing into his side. He reached down, pulled the offending booklet from his pocket and settled down to sleep.

When he opened his eyes, the Green Line Coach Guide was resting precariously on his lap. He sat up. The Guide fell to the floor, and a small rectangle of paper spilled from it and sailed into the gangway. He leaned over to pick it up and found that it was a newspaper clipping. Still half asleep, he glanced at it and saw that it was in English, the review of some art show or other at one of the London galleries.

That was all right. That was in the character of Kusitch. The ex-dealer was interested in the current exhibitions. He would take advantage of his mission to England to see what was going on. No doubt he had clipped this piece from some weekly journal as a reminder. The Blandish Gallery . . . twelve new works . . .

He came fully awake, realising the implication of his find. This clipping had been placed between the pages of the Guide, and, back in the bedroom at the Risler-Moircy, he had failed to discover it. There might be other things concealed in that booklet of Green Line timetables.

He recovered the Guide from the floor and began to go through it page by page. He found nothing until he came to the Guildford-London-Hertford route. Here, a line was drawn in ink under the coach times given for Oxford Circus and a question mark had been placed in the margin against the Turkey Street stopping point. Or possibly it applied to the next point, Waltham Cross. It was difficult to decide. Above the timetable, also in ink, were the letters and figures SS 729. Below, an address was scrawled in pencil. It looked like Walden or Wallen House, Cheriton Shawe, Hertford.

He plodded on to the end of the booklet, eager for further finds, but there was nothing else. He turned back. The Cheriton Shawe address might be a place to stay at, or the residence of someone Kusitch had been instructed to see. The suggestion that Kusitch had planned to use the Green Line bus made the possession of the Guide intelligible enough, but it certainly did nothing to explain why he had taken the trouble to hide so innocent a publication under the carpet. Perhaps the key to everything was in that SS 729, but the cryptogram could not be read merely by looking at it.

Andrew went back to the press clipping. This time he read it attentively, but the second sentence pulled him up, and he stared at the piece of paper as if he could not trust his eyes. He stared at it for quite a time, thinking hard. Then he went back to the beginning and read it right through. The Blandish Gallery, that Delphian temple of the *avant garde,* is presenting twelve new works which it somewhat recklessly describes as sculptures. We have had, in the past, some acquaintance with Ruth Meriden, but we were not quite prepared for the development displayed in these latest *facettes* of her art. Abjuring her rigid acceptance of Naum Gabo as the one source of pure light, she is discovering something within herself. We say "something" advisedly. She has not yet cast off the chains of eclecticism, but the discerning must admit that this new empiric phase is interesting, combining as it does the *brio* of a Brancusi, the *mièvrerie* of a Meštrovi with the cool *mathématique* of the aforementioned Russian master. Miss Meriden is young. She has still much to learn. But in some of these twelve works she displays an aptitude in the handling of her recessions, and we also find an encouraging restlessness, a reaching down towards a firmer *enfoncement.* We like most of all the piece defined as Etude Opus 5. There is here a striving towards an existentialist concept that Sartre himself might applaud. The introductory note in the catalogue describes it as Mozartean. We do not concur. The melodic line is more in the tradition of Scarlatti.

Andrew felt confused. He could not at once decide whether the girl with the red hair was a sculptor or a composer, but, when he weighed the evidence, the balance turned against music. Gabo, Brancusi and Meštrovi were ponderable witnesses, or so it seemed, that Ruth Meriden was a sculptor of sorts. Ruth Meriden . . .

He meditated. It was strange how the girl kept bobbing up.

Strange, or not strange . . . ?

He had an idea then that made him jump. Ruth Meriden had joined the Brussels plane at Athens. So had Kusitch. Ruth Meriden had stayed the night in Brussels at the Risler-Moircy. Kusitch had held out till he and Andrew had been given a suite at the same hotel. And now, from the booklet that Kusitch had hidden, came this newspaper clipping about Ruth Meriden. So?

There was no answer.

Andrew opened the Green Line Guide again and gazed at the cryptogram above the London-Bishops Stortford timetable.

SS 729.

When he looked out of the window a few minutes later, the plane was over England.

Five

AFTER THE FIRST twenty-four hours London seemed curiously empty. Andrew was still doing the things he had long dreamed of doing; seeing the places that, in Thessaly, had sometimes appeared as remote as Everest or Xanadu. To cross Piccadilly Circus had become an enormous ambition; let him but see Charing Cross Station again and stout Cortez could have the Pacific. But, of course, the reality was less satisfactory. The joys of homecoming were somehow superficial. He felt restless and vaguely uneasy. Never before had he had with quite such intensity the feeling that there was something missing.

If this was to be the mood of the maturer Maclaren, he could regret the loss of the more youthful exuberance that had sent him to his European experiences without a thought for his own interests. Of course, he was alone in the world; but then, he always had been. Now it was like coming back to search among scattered ruins for a lost past and discovering that after all there was nothing to be retrieved.

There had been no relatives on hand to greet him. His mother had died while he was still a student at Edinburgh. His father had accepted an important medical post in the Pacific during the war and had stayed on out there to continue research in tropical diseases. He had some uncles and aunts and innumerable cousins, but, even if he had been interested in them, none was in London.

He had good friends who were delighted to see him again and

eager to help him. He had arranged to stay with one of them until he found accommodation, but the expected meeting had been postponed. Roger Lang had rushed off to America, leaving a hurried note and the keys of his flat in Holland Park, but this disappointment had nothing to do with his mood. He had other friends and they welcomed him warmly enough. Some of them frankly envied him; and really he had to admit that he was not out of luck. Home again, a comfortable flat to live in, a month of freedom, and then work that he wanted to do, with the promise of a specialist's career in the future.

There had been a note awaiting him, asking him to call up Dr. Jeffrey at the Kingsland Road Eye Hospital as soon as he arrived.

The old man said: "Hello, son! Got in a day late, didn't you? What put this bee in your bonnet about glaucoma?"

"It was thrown at me, sir. Quite a few cases in some parts of Greece."

"Carotene deficiency. Xerophthalmis breaking out all over the place. They will have their damn silly wars."

Andrew smiled. "It's wonderful to think I'll be working with you, sir."

"Save that for a few months. Wait till you find out what it's like to be a registrar at this madhouse."

"I'm grateful to you for the job."

"You wouldn't have got it if I hadn't thought I could use you. Don't run away with the notion that you've been favoured because of your father. What you wrote about intraocular pressure happened to interest me. Look in on me next week sometime. We'll discuss procedure. You'll have every opportunity to work out your ideas. Meanwhile, enjoy your holiday."

After three days of it the month ahead of him began to look like eternity. He thought of asking old Jeffrey if he couldn't start work earlier, but he suspected it would be impossible. The hospital had been emphatic about the date of the vacancy. Another man was moving on. Andrew would have to wait till the discarded shoes were ready for him.

Nothing to do on a sunny morning but shop for socks and a couple of preposterously expensive shirts. The prices of clothes depressed him. Or something did. He wished he hadn't come home. He wished he had stayed in Larissa another week or so. If he had put off the trip till a more reasonable date, he wouldn't have encountered Pyotr Grigorievitch Kusitch or be wandering along Bond Street on this bright day plagued by anxiety about the little man. Anxiety? Or simply the tantalising probability that he would never know for certain whether the little man had been the central figure in a melodrama or just plain mad?

He turned left into Oxford Street, descended the stairway of the first underground station, bought a ticket, and stepped onto the escalator. He did it all reluctantly, under some inward protest. His mood went down, down, down with the moving stairway. Then he touched bottom, and his mind suddenly cleared. He walked round and stepped onto the ascending escalator. He thrust his ticket into the hand of the collector and hurried on, afraid that the man might challenge him. He hadn't used a train, yet he had a feeling of guilt, as if he had broken a contract with the London Transport Executive. He hurried away from the scene of the crime towards the telephone booths. He took up the directory A-D, and flicked over the leaves. Bla . . . Blan . . . Blandish! His moving finger halted. He made a mental note of an address and walked out into the sunlight again.

For the first time since his homecoming, he felt like a man with a purpose. He swung round one corner, strode on, turned another corner, and slowed a little, noting the numbers. The odds were on one side, the evens on another. He crossed the road. A few more paces and he was there.

The Blandish Gallery had an elegant front. It had a beautiful door of burnished bronze and one small Dufy in a large window. A hand-lettered placard in a bronze frame announced an exhibition of water colours by Christophe Chambord.

Andrew Maclaren had the sensation of something inside him

dropping with the gravitational abandon of a plummet. It was something extraphysical, something completely unscientific and quite beyond material diagnosis. You could approach it only through the figurative. It was as the falling stick of a spent rocket. It was the dead meteor hope.

The exhibition of sculptures by Ruth Meriden was over. The press notice preserved by Kusitch might have been clipped a month ago or a year ago; it was all the same now. Andrew went back gloomily to the tube station and bought another ticket.

When he let himself into the flat, he saw the Green Line Coach Guide lying on Roger Lang's desk. He picked it up and threw it into Roger Lang's wastebasket.

That was that!

He almost spoke it aloud to put the finality of it beyond question. He was finished with Kusitch; Ruth Meriden was expunged from his mind. He poured himself a drink to celebrate the liberation. After a second drink he crossed to the wastebasket and recovered the Coach Guide. He opened it at the marked page and stared at the cryptogram, but all he found in it was a resolute determination to be meaningless. He was sure it was something simple, possibly absurdly simple. The trouble was he had no knowledge of such things. They were a special study. They required an unusual aptitude, a sort of . . .

And then inspiration came.

Charley Botten!

He blinked. He looked up another telephone number and then realised that he could do nothing about it till after office hours. He paced Roger Lang's carpet till darkness came. At the first feasible moment he dialled the number, and miraculously the receiver at the other end was lifted.

"Charley?" he demanded. "This is Andrew Maclaren; remember? I've just got back from Athens."

Mr. Botten said: "How are things in Greece?" He didn't sound as if he cared.

Andrew decided that the question was not one he need answer. He asked: "Are you still in M.I. five?" "Resigned years ago," Charley answered. "I'm in business. Anyway it wasn't M.I. five."

"What I really mean is do you still go in for ciphers and puzzles and things?"

"Certainly. I'm a stockbroker. What can I do for you?"

"I want to see you urgently. May I call? I've got something I can't make out."

"So have I. I think it's ulcers but it may be a delayed hangover. Come along at once."

Face to face with his caller, Mr. Botten was more cordial. He listened to some account of Mr. Kusitch and then examined the enigma in the Coach Guide. He was an expert of experts; he had volumes of information in his head and quite a small library within reach, but he shook his head over that SS 729.

"You say this fellow Kusitch tracks down war loot?" he said. "If that's true, this sequence may be merely the catalogue number of a museum piece."

"I don't know," Andrew answered. "I think there's more to it. I think it's the thing he wanted to hide, though why he should write it down if it means anything dangerous, I can't make out. He could have memorised it."

"Probably no head for figures." Mr. Botten laughed with the good-natured tolerance of those who have no heads for anything else. "Let's look at it this way. He makes these notes in the Guide, thinking they'll be safe enough in the normal course. Then he is forced off the normal course when he has to spend the night in Brussels. Suddenly, while you're preparing to go out to dine, he remembers the Guide, gets a bit nervous about it, and shoves it under the carpet. It may be not all that important, but he doesn't want to carry it on him or have anyone fool round with it while he's absent. Didn't he give you any hint about it in his talk?"

"Nothing that I can remember, except that he lives in Dubrovnik, or did."

"What has that to do with it?"

"Probably nothing. Dubrovnik's a port." "I'm quite aware of that. Where's the connection?"

"I did think at first that the SS might stand for steamship."

"It might stand for Schutzstaffel. The figures could represent a unit or a regimental number. It ties up with the Nazis and their loot."

Andrew objected. "I've an idea it has something to do with this country; that it ties up with the address and the timetable."

Charley Botten wrote the symbols down on the back of an envelope and glared at them.

"I can't get the idea of this search for loot out of my head," he said. "The catalogue number is quite feasible. The SS could be a sign for sculptures. What's the matter?"

"Nothing." He had not said anything about Ruth Meriden or the review of her show, and he was reluctant to start on further explanations. "You're probably right," he said. "No doubt Kusitch had to deal with sculptures."

"He also had to deal with thugs. If I were you, chum, I'd forget all about the business. If something has happened to your pal Kusitch you don't want it happening to you."

Andrew laughed. "You were too long with M.I. whatever-it-is. If you're not careful, you'll be seeing cloak-and-dagger men round every dark corner."

"A few days ago you were seeing them in Brussels in broad daylight."

"They gave up when I went to the police."

"That's what you think. I wouldn't be too sure."

"Anyway, that was Brussels."

"And this is London. Splendid! If the prospect doesn't appal you, let's go out and sample some English cooking. Unless you'd prefer a moussaka? You're dining with me."

It was after eleven when the two parted and Mr. Botten's hangover had been treated. Andrew took the Central Line to

Holland Park, and came up in the lift with quite a crowd of passengers. He liked the underground. It was home, it was London. For the first time since his return he had the feeling of being absorbed by the throng. These people who pressed into the lift were Londoners. They couldn't be anything else. They conveyed to him a friendliness from which he had been away too long. Charley Botten would say it was all imagination, or sentimentality. He would deny that London was any safer than Brussels, but Charley had become cynical. That war job of his had warped him, distorted his perspective. How could one not feel safe among these friendly people? Of course they might murder one another occasionally, but not in the underground, not in crowded lifts or busy streets. Not very often, anyway. This was London.

Andrew maintained the lyrical mood for a couple of hundred yards along Holland Park Avenue. Then, as he waited to cross the road, he had a twinge of uneasiness. There was a man on the curb a few yards away from him, and Andrew could have sworn that he had seen the same fellow in the lift. One of the friendly ones; a jolly-faced man of forty-five or so with smiling eyes; a small man, getting portly. When the traffic lights changed, he crossed the road behind Andrew, but surely there was nothing in that to worry about? It was a free road. Anyone could choose which side he walked on.

The friendly one loitered at a bus stop for a moment or two, but merely to light a cigarette. When Andrew looked back, he was about fifty yards behind. Andrew turned off the main road. Instead of going on along the avenue, Jolly-Face turned, too, and, by the time he rounded the next corner, he had closed the gap a little.

It was absurd to think there was anything in it. Plenty of people lived in Holland Park; quite a lot in Pemberley Crescent, and Jolly-Face could be one of them.

This was London. Unworthy suspicion must be banished. It arose, of course, as a result of the Brussels incident and the melodramatic nonsense of Charley Botten.

Andrew tried to clear his mind of the nonsense, but every time he looked back the man was still there, and there was no one else in sight. Not another soul in all the long street.

A few more yards and Andrew could no longer frame arguments to counter his uneasiness. A few more and the situation was no longer merely odd; it was a little frightening. There was a stretch now where a street lamp had failed. There were shadows under overhanging trees. There were lightless houses and dark, ominous gardens behind closed gates. Andrew fought against a desire to accelerate his pace. He heard the footsteps coming along behind him, keeping an even distance. One shoe rasped slightly with each step as if a metal protector had been driven into the sole. Except for their footsteps, the two progressed in a pocket of silence. The noise of traffic along Holland Park Avenue was a distant murmur, and the two moved on into deeper silence. Not a single car came round the curve of Pemberley Crescent. The next time Andrew looked back he saw the man throw away his cigarette. It tossed up a little spray of sparks when it hit the roadway.

Then Jolly-Face began to whistle a tune, and he repeated it over and over. At first Andrew could not identify it; after a few repetitions he recognised it as a phrase from *Till Eulenspiegel*. The whistler was trying to work it up into something, but he was not very musical.

The tension in Andrew eased. That human trick of whistling seemed to make the fellow less formidable. And Andrew was also comforted by the thought that there were only a few more yards to go. Then, with an accession of confidence, he wondered if he should go on, past the house. If the whistler were really following him, it must be to mark where he lived, for the man had made no attempt to catch up with him.

For a moment Andrew thought of going back to Holland Park Avenue and leading the fellow a chase by bus and tube and taxi with the object of throwing him off. He was in front of the house now. He hesitated. Light from the hall came dimly through the ribbed glass panels of the heavy door. Shadows moved in front of the panels and two men came down the steps. There was no longer any choice for Andrew. He knew the taller of the two men at once, and the recognition left him rigid, momentarily incapable of movement. He stood with one foot advanced, waiting, staring. Inspector Jordaens wore a sparely cut raincoat that had the effect of emphasising his leanness, and his hat—a black felt with a high crown and a very narrow brim—conveyed an immediate suggestion of something alien. He raised it courteously.

"Good evening, Dr. Maclaren. We have been waiting for you for some time."

As Andrew moved forward Jolly-Face passed. He stopped whistling and glanced at the three figures on the steps. Then he was gone. A few yards beyond the house he resumed his musical experiment. The rhythmic theme from *Till Eulenspiegel* died away in the distance.

Inspector Jordaens introduced the shorter man. "This is my friend Detective-Sergeant Stock of Scotland Yard. We have been trying to make contact with you all the evening, Dr. Maclaren."

It did not take any special gift to know what was coming. Andrew could have shaped the answer for himself as he asked the obvious question.

"What do you want with me?"

"Perhaps you will be good enough to invite us inside. It is about your friend Kusitch. His body was found in the Bois de la Cambre early this morning. I have been studying very closely the statement you gave me in Brussels. I wish to ask you some more questions."

Six

INSPECTOR JORDAENS was a very painstaking man. It was after three o'clock in the morning before he left.

Kusitch had been shot through the head but other, less pleasant, things had happened to him first. Jordaens had a theory but it only made things more mystifying. The kidnappers, he thought, had not taken Kusitch from the hotel bedroom merely to murder him. If that had been their aim, they could have accomplished it without going to all the trouble of smuggling the man out of the Risler-Moircy. And with less risk, the Inspector insisted.

No. It was obvious that Kusitch had been abducted because he possessed some information that the assassins wanted.

"What was that information, Dr. Maclaren?"

Something in the tone, or it may have been in the impassive air of Jordaens, irritated Andrew.

"How should I know? I was not one of the assassins."

"According to our knowledge, you were the last person to talk to this man; the last to see him alive."

"Except for the assassins."

"Assuredly, except for the assassins. The peculiarity, Dr. Maclaren, is that you came to me with the fear that Kusitch was in grave danger."

"If there is any peculiarity, Inspector, it is that you would not listen to me."

"Ah, please, Doctor!" Jordaens rustled his notes of the interview

58

at the Commissariat. "But you wouldn't," Andrew insisted. "You rejected the idea completely."

"What convinced you that there was danger?"

"I wasn't convinced. I told you my reasons: the man's behaviour, his fear of enemies."

"Did you tell me everything?"

"Of course I told you everything. Why shouldn't I have told you?"

"Exactly, Dr. Maclaren. Why?"

The Inspector was watching him with narrowed eyes. The Scotland Yard man was staring gloomily at the carpet.

Andrew experienced a momentary guilty panic. Then he lost his temper. He stood up quickly.

"If you think I had anything to do with it, why don't you say so?"

The challenge had a startling effect. The Scotland Yard man's head jerked up. The Inspector looked deeply shocked. It was as if some unacceptable obscenity had been uttered. There was a moment's embarrassing silence, and then Andrew turned away and poured himself another drink. He heard a faint sigh of exasperation from the Belgian.

"My dear Doctor," said Jordaens primly, "you misunderstand. Naturally, your own movements have been closely checked. I am quite satisfied that you were here in England at least twenty-four hours before Kusitch died."

Andrew sat down again. Inspector Jordaens regarded him coldly.

"I merely asked a question, Dr. Maclaren."

"I beg your pardon," Andrew said, "I thought you were cross-examining."

"Please concentrate, Dr. Maclaren. It is a very important point. Are you sure there is nothing you missed in your statement to me? Some little detail, for instance, that may be enlarged by the knowledge you now possess?"

Andrew wanted time to consider. Except for the detail of the Coach Guide, he was sure there was nothing he had withheld, but the Coach Guide had become the all-important factor. He sipped his drink. The man from Scotland Yard was staring at him with expressionless eyes. Jordaens cleared his throat.

"I want you to think hard, Dr. Maclaren. You collected the articles left in the bathroom. Did it not occur to you to look in the bedroom for other things that Kusitch might have neglected?"

"I glanced round when I entered from the corridor. I saw nothing.

"That was the first time you entered the bedroom."

"I made that quite clear in my Brussels statement."

The Inspector made the pages of the statement rustle again. "Yes, I see you did," he agreed. "Yes, yes." Reading, he turned the pages. Then he looked up sharply.

"I have it that you went back to the hotel from the air terminal after cancelling your seat on the morning plane."

"Yes."

The Inspector went on reading. An itch ran over Andrew's body in the intolerable pause.

"Exactly." Jordaens cleared his throat again. "You went back to see if any word had come in from Kusitch. Is that right?"

"Yes."

"We have since had talks with the hotel staff. You revisited the bedroom, saying you had forgotten something. You entered by way of the bathroom and bolted the door against the chambermaid. Why did you do that?"

"I didn't want the maid to follow me. I had an idea that Kusitch might have been murdered in his room. I wanted to look in the clothes cupboard."

"So!" Jordaens forced a small measure of geniality into his voice. "I was sure you would have a perfectly reasonable explanation. But why not say?"

Andrew had a deep mistrust of that affability. He answered

sharply, "I didn't see what there was to say. It was absurd, the idea of expecting to find a body in the cupboard."

"Possibly." The Inspector shrugged away this lay opinion. "Am I then to understand that you had no other reason for revisiting the bedroom?"

"No. There was another reason."

It had to come out now. He must hand over the Coach Guide. The circumstance of murder made that imperative. For better or worse, Inspector Jordaens was the man in charge of the investigation.

"Yes, Dr. Maclaren?"

"I had remembered something," Andrew confessed. "I saw Kusitch push an envelope under the carpet in his room. I wanted to see if it was still there. I thought it might contain money. I believed that if it were no longer there it would be proof that Kusitch had left of his own free will."

There was a silence and, for Andrew, an accusation in every moment of it.

"It was there," he said. "But it wasn't what I expected. It was an English timetable, for the Green Line coaches."

The Scotland Yard man made a movement. A gleam of interest showed in his eyes.

Jordaens was severe. "Why did you not tell me of this in Brussels?"

"Because you treated me as if I had been imagining things."

"An entirely false impression. I cannot accept it, Dr. Maclaren."

"I don't care a damn whether you accept it or not," Andrew said calmly, "I'm telling you the facts. I thought myself that this business of the Coach Guide was fantastic. I was afraid you would dismiss the whole story if I told you about it."

"What has become of the Coach Guide? I hope you are not about to tell me that you threw it away?"

Andrew took it from his pocket and handed it over. "You'll find some marks on page one-three-eight," he said. "And this was inside it." He produced the art criticism from his wallet. "I wasn't aware of it till I was on the plane for London," he added.

Jordaens studied the page, then read the cutting. Detective-Sergeant Stock was interested enough to rise and look over the Belgian's shoulder.

"Ruth Meriden!" the Inspector exclaimed. "That is the name of the woman who was on the plane from Athens. She proceeded by the morning flight to London." He referred to his notebook. "Also, she stayed at the Hotel Risler-Moircy. You knew that, Dr. Maclaren?"

"Yes." Andrew felt uncomfortable under the probing gaze. "It's curious," he added.

"We learn, my gifted colleague and I, that things so reasonable and logical are not to be characterised as curious."

The gifted colleague, back in his chair, nodded glumly.

"The Risler-Moircy," Jordaens announced, "was one of the few hotels that could offer accommodation to the air line. Therefore, you will be wrong, Dr. Maclaren, to conjure on the theme of a contrived coincidence."

"I'm not conjuring on anything," Andrew said irritably. "I just think it's curious that Kusitch should have had in his possession that cutting about a fellow passenger."

"But what is more likely? Kusitch is interested in art. This lady is an artist. He is on his way to England. Perhaps he hopes to see her work, to become acquainted. He has noticed her name on the list of passengers, and"—the Inspector produced a rather astonishing leer—"I understand the lady is quite personable. You observed that yourself, Dr. Maclaren?"

"Yes, I did. All right then, the cutting's unimportant."

"It may be so. You knew this lady?"

"I don't know anything about her."

"No? You did not even speak to her?"

Andrew felt a tightening sensation in his stomach.

"I spoke to her at the airport, if that's what you mean. She seemed to be in some difficulty with a porter. I offered my help."

"As you might have done to any lady in distress, young or old." Jordaens achieved a dry chuckle. "By coincidence, your little encounter was observed. We have always a detective on duty at the airport. By another coincidence, the same man was given the task of guarding you when you left my office. He remembered you."

There were enough coincidences to bring a prickle of sweat to Andrew's scalp.

Jordaens nodded comfortably.

"On an air journey one finds opportunities," he commented. "It would seem that Mr. Kusitch was diligent enough to acquire Miss Meriden's address." He read the scrawl on the timetable. "Walden House, Cheriton Shawe, Hertfordshire. We shall see. We are investigating Miss Meriden in due course. Just as a matter of routine. We wish to question all the passengers who may have observed Kusitch or had contact with him."

"He had no contact with the girl on the flight from Athens," Andrew said.

"No doubt he was biding his time." Jordaens brought the leer into play again for a moment. Then it vanished and he turned to Stock. "This inscription at the top, SS seven-two-nine—it could be a telephone number, no?"

"No." The man from Scotland Yard was emphatic.

"Perhaps Dr. Maclaren has an explanation?"

"No. But, as a matter of fact, I did take it to an expert."

"An expert? You have been doing some detective work yourself?" He turned to exchange glances with Scotland Yard. "England!" His hands flowed eloquently in the air. "The land of the *roman policier,* where every citizen is a policeman. And what did your expert conclude, Dr. Maclaren?"

"He didn't conclude anything. He thinks the symbols may be the catalogue number of some sculpture."

"Exactly my own thought. A catalogue number of an item by the personable Miss Meriden." He put the clipping and the Coach

Guide down on a coffee table at his side, rejecting, if not entirely spurning them. "Now let us be serious, Dr. Maclaren. I want you to make every effort to remember. Was there not something, a gesture, a sign, a little word from Kusitch, that would give us a clue to the purpose of his journey to England?" "I have told you, Inspector. His job was to track down war loot for his country."

"We have been in touch with the Yugoslav authorities." Jordaens managed to convey that those who gave information could expect to receive some in return. "What you say about his job is true. We learned that he had been quite successful at it. He was known favourably to important officers of the occupation in Germany and Austria, and, indeed, had had some acquaintance with my own superiors. There can be no question of his commission in general. It was authentic. He came and went for his government. But there seems to be considerable doubt, some mystery, about his final movements. He told you, Dr. Maclaren, that he had work to do in England. Are you sure he didn't mention the nature of the work?"

"Positive. He was evasive about his trip. When I pressed him he said he had told me enough."

"I thought so. It is all in accord."

This satisfaction over negative evidence was puzzling.

"In accord with what?" Andrew asked.

Jordaens hesitated briefly, then made up his mind. "I think I may confide in you, Dr. Maclaren. The Yugoslav authorities were quite frank with us. Last week Kusitch applied to his superiors for a permit to go to Greece. He had, he said, information about some missing icons of great value. There was no reason to doubt his claim; he had proved his good faith many times. He was sent to Athens to investigate, and there, so far as Yugoslavia is concerned, he disappeared. What he did, from the time he reached Athens, was on his own responsibility and for himself. When he failed to report to an agent in Athens, he was set down as a deserter. The authorities are now satisfied that the icons never were in Greece. Kusitch ended his life as an absconder, a fugitive, misappropriating his expense money."

Andrew remembered his own reservations about Kusitch's good faith; but there were other factors.

"What about his wife and child in Dubrovnik?" he asked.

"The child does not exist. The wife he deserted years ago. She has now put forward the belief that Kusitch always wanted to establish himself again as an art dealer; that he made this opportunity to leave Yugoslavia for good."

"With enough money for his purpose?" Andrew was incredulous.

"You are right to be sceptical," Jordaens conceded. "He had little more than enough to take him to England. It is very mystifying. My own theory is that he had found some art treasure on a previous excursion; that he had sent it to England instead of restoring it to his country; that he deserted with the hope of selling his treasure. We do not know why he was murdered, but it is not impossible to imagine that he was involved with some dangerous types."

Andrew remembered Kusitch's own words. *"It is inevitable in my trade that I make enemies."* But how could these enemies have known that he would spend that one night in Brussels? They—or one of them at least—must have been on the plane from Athens, keeping Kusitch in sight.

He put the question to Jordaens, who was ready with an answer. The assassins had been advised from Athens that Kusitch was a passenger to England. They had intended to pick him up on the Brussels-to-London flight that night, but the fog had revised their plans.

"This is the hypothesis," Jordaens said. "It is supported circumstantially. Two men secured passage on the London plane in the afternoon. When the flight was cancelled, they demanded their money back; they said they would go by sea. They gave the names of Kretchmann and Haller. They were at the airport when your plane arrived from Athens. They did, in fact, leave by sea, but only yesterday. Had they delayed a few more hours, it might have been very difficult for them. We thought at first that one of them might have been the man following you in Brussels, but your description did not tally."

"I was followed tonight, from the Holland Park tube station," Andrew asserted. "You might have seen the fellow if you were observant. When you and Sergeant Stock came down the steps outside, he walked on past the house."

The Inspector raised his eyebrows. "The cheerful-looking man who was whistling Strauss with a most imperfect ear?"

"Yes." Andrew was surprised at this evidence of the Inspector's acumen. His voice must have revealed the fact. The Inspector smiled.

"I have no wish to cast doubts, Dr. Maclaren. You are, I have remarked, a very intelligent man. As an intelligent man you would, of course, be careful to see that you did not allow yourself to be too much influenced by your imagination. Do you understand?"

Dr. Maclaren understood perfectly. He was being told not to be a timid fool; that no one had followed him from the Holland Park tube.

"In any case," the Inspector added, "your Mr. Eulenspiegel was neither Kretchmann nor Haller. The one is very tall, with a spare frame; the other, Haller, is of medium height, heavily built. And I may tell you that they are very dangerous men. We know something of them in my department. They were in the German Army, and when the break up came they gave us trouble. There was a gang of them, with Kretchmann as their leader. We had Kretchmann and Haller in the box for a while. Later we pushed them across the frontier, but they returned to give us more trouble. Yes, Dr. Maclaren, I must impress on you that they are very dangerous men, and it would be exceedingly foolish for you to become involved with them."

"Involved?"

"We believe these men have come to England and we are now trying to trace them through our good friends at Scotland Yard.

They may have other names and false passports, but they will be just as dangerous. Be warned." He wagged a finger roguishly and smiled. Then the smile went out. "And now, Doctor, I think we should go over your Brussels statement line by line. You may recall something fresh; an omission, perhaps, or a valuable thought." "I've told you of all that happened," Andrew protested. "I've given you the Coach Guide. There's a clue for you."

"What makes you think it is a clue?"

"Why should Kusitch have hidden it under the carpet if it were not important to him?"

Sergeant Stock reached across the coffee table for the Coach Guide, studied it as if he were intent on getting somewhere, then put it back on the table.

"It has come within my observation," said the Inspector pompously, "that the mind of the secret agent acts in peculiar ways. Possibly Kusitch was used to hiding things under carpets. He did not wish to carry the Guide with him, so . . ." He shrugged. "A timetable with an address, the catalogue number of a work of art, a pretty young girl, a secretive Yugoslav!" The Inspector was tolerant of human frailty. "Kusitch may have been jealous of you, Dr. Maclaren. He wished to retain the lady's address for his own use."

"I tell you the thing is important," Andrew retorted. "It means something."

"My dear Dr. Maclaren!" He was jocular now. "I yield place to no man in my admiration of your great Sherlock Holmes. I enjoy the exploits of your many justly famous private investigators, but you, as a man of science, should realise the weakness of intuitive reasoning." He looked to Detective-Sergeant Stock for approval, and received a nod. "No, Dr. Maclaren. In police work we need facts, not fancies. A man has been murdered. I have in my possession the bullet with which he was slain. Find me the pistol from which that bullet came, and then we may be near to the hand that pulled the trigger. Meanwhile let us consider again your deposition."

It was after three before it was over. Jordaens said: "I am afraid

Detective-Sergeant Stock is growing tired. You look rather weary yourself, Dr. Maclaren. If there is anything else, we will communicate. Meanwhile, you had better get some sleep."

The advice was not difficult to follow. As soon as they had gone he got into bed and was asleep before he could stretch out. Then, in a few minutes it seemed, the sun was streaming in and the doorbell was ringing. He cursed and turned over, but the doorbell was persistent. He got into his dressing gown, expecting a telegram or registered letter. It was neither. It was Charley Botten.

"Sleeping late?" Charley asked. "Or am I so early? Sorry if I've disturbed you, but I thought I'd look in on my way to the office. I had a brain wave about your riddle when I got home to the flat."

Interest was slow to revive. "Come in," Andrew said. "I'll put on some coffee."

"I should have recognised from the start that those symbols were the registration number of a fishing craft," Charley said. "Perhaps it was just too simple."

Andrew came fully awake. His jerking hand spilled ground coffee on the gas stove.

"Fishing craft!" he exclaimed.

"I had to do with them during the war," Charley said. "I remembered that SS stood for St. Ives, so I telephoned to a man in Cornwall. I got quite a lot of information, and it ties up with Dubrovnik."

Andrew forgot the coffee. Mr. Botten produced a page from a telephone pad on which he had made some notes.

"This friend in Cornwall called me back first thing this morning," he explained. "The registration number tallies with a local craft, thirty foot long with a nine-foot beam. Her first owner was a man named Gurley and he bought her in the early twenties. Apparently she was quite well known round St. Ives as the *Mary Isabella,* a nice little job with a handy yawl rig and an auxiliary engine. Gurley did very well out of her for some years. Then things went wrong and finally he had to sell up everything he had. The yawl was in pretty bad shape by that time, and a couple of Falmouth youngsters—Jim and Dan Pascoe—bought her for a very small figure."

"What's the link with Dubrovnik?" Andrew demanded.

"I'm coming to that. It happened that my friend remembered the craft. He got Dan Pascoe on the phone and heard the rest of it. The boys bought the tub in 1938. They spent all the winter repairing her and fitting her out for a cruise, and next spring and summer they took her round Spain, through the Mediterranean to the Adriatic, and along the Dalmatian Coast."

"Yugoslavia!" Andrew was conscious of the coffee percolator spouting behind him, but ignored it.

"Getting hot, isn't it?" Charley Botten grinned. "The Pascoes ended their cruise at a place called Zavrana. That's a few miles up the coast from Dubrovnik, if I know my geography. They had storm damage. They were afraid to tackle the return voyage without proper repairs. They gave the job to a small yard at Zavrana. Then it looked as if the war was going to break at any minute, and they wanted to get home as they were on the reserve. There was a motor yacht in the port, owned by a crazy Englishman with money to burn. The Pascoes got acquainted with him and sold him the yawl. It seems he had some cockeyed idea of using it as a tender for his yacht. Mad as a bandicoot. Wouldn't hear of war. Had just bought a palace up in the hills behind Zavrana. The Pascoes came home by air. That's the end of the story. They don't know what happened to the yawl."

Andrew was pacing the floor.

"Did your friend get the name of the Englishman, the fellow who bought the yawl?" he asked.

"Meriden," Charley answered. "John Quayle Meriden. What's the matter now?"

Andrew had the sensation of something bumping inside him. He didn't like it. It was all very unprofessional, and the worst of it was he couldn't control himself.

"There's nothing the matter," he answered. "I was just wondering why Kusitch had the number of this yawl."

"Do you know Meriden? You jumped at the mention of him."

"Just a coincidence." Andrew struggled to give an appearance of nonchalance. "Someone of the same name. Couldn't possibly be related. After all, it's quite a common name."

"Sure," Charley agreed. "There's this fellow with the yacht, and then there's a place called Meriden in Connecticut. I went to all the trouble and expense of calling Dan Pascoe myself to find out if this John Quayle had given him any address. He had. I'll let you have two guesses."

"Cheriton Shawe."

"You don't need the second one. Your coffee's boiling over."

"I'll get you a cup."

"Thanks, I've had some. I have to be on my way."

"Do you mind letting me have your notes on the yawl?"

"Not at all, if you can forgive the doodling." He handed over the page from the pad. "Now that your puzzle is solved, Maclaren, you'd better forget all about it. Kusitch obviously had some business to transact over the yawl. He'll turn up all right."

"Kusitch is dead, murdered."

Botten stared and asked questions. Andrew supplied the facts. Botten looked grave. "Keep your nose out of it," he said. "Murder is a job for the police. They don't take kindly to amateur interference. Neither do ex-SS men. You drink your coffee and forget about it."

When he was alone Andrew examined the sheet from the telephone pad. It read:

SS 729—Mary Isabella—yawl 30 x 9 Gurley early twenties Gurley early Gurley auxiliary yes yes yes. NO!!! Sold Fal Pascoes Jimdan sailed Dubrovnik Zavrana. Bought for tender Englishman Jno. Quail Meriden— Quayle—to motor yacht. Repairs, war, last heard. Pascoes air-flighted home. War, war, war—God knows.

It was all there if you knew how to translate it. Andrew read it a second time as he prepared to shave. Then he thrust the scrap of paper into a pocket of his dressing gown.

The advice to keep his nose out of it was undoubtedly sound, and Jordaens would agree that the job was exclusively for the police, but leave it to Jordaens and it would never be done. The man was an ass. Imagine his reaction if he were now told about the yawl-rigged fishing craft that had been sailed down to Zavrana and there sold to John Quayle Meriden! Another ponderous homily on private investigators, no doubt.

"What, more of your expert, Dr. Maclaren? Ah, England, England! Where would we be without your detective stories? This is very clever, Dr. Maclaren, but it is not police work. Pyotr Grigorievitch Kusitch was not killed with a yawl-rigged fishing craft. The main issue is unaffected by the suggestion that he was making inquiries for Mr. Meriden about his lost tender. Find me Kretchmann and Haller, Dr. Maclaren! Find me Kretchmann and Haller. . . ."

Perhaps he would. He vowed, as he finished dressing, that he was certainly going to find out some more about the mysterious yawl before he volunteered any further information to Inspector Jordaens and Stock. He'd make them take notice of him before he was done with the case.

The annoying thing was that, in spite of his obvious contempt for the Coach Guide as a clue, Inspector Jordaens had insisted on taking it away with him. He had taken the cutting about Ruth Meriden, too.

As soon as he had bathed and dressed, Andrew went out and bought another copy of the Coach Guide. Then he looked up Cheriton Shawe on the map.

Seven

ON THE MAP, Cheriton Shawe looked like a small village not far from the Hertford Road. It appeared to be some distance off the coach route, but, short of hiring a car to get there, the Green Line Coach seemed to be the best means of reaching it. The nearest railway station was several miles away.

The coach was comfortable. It made good speed. And the conductor knew all about the way to get to Cheriton Shawe. "Your best route, sir, is by Wyminden Lane. That's before we come to Waltham Cross."

London sprawled out over the morning till you might have thought the suburbs reached to Aberdeen. They seemed endless. The road bent, squirmed, curved, shot off at tangents and doubled back on itself; but the coach knew its business. It got there.

"Wyminden Lane," the conductor called.

Green patches had been a little more frequent among the bricks and mortar. At Wyminden Lane you had the feeling of being on the edge of town. There were houses on one side of the main road, fields on the other; and the lane, wide and newly paved, reached flatly out across the fields.

The coach sped on, leaving its one alighting passenger to a sense of loneliness and dismay. The hope he had had of picking up a taxi was immediately dashed. There was not a vehicle in sight, or any sign of a garage. Possibly he would find something along the lane. If not, it wasn't far to Cheriton Shawe.

After walking for ten minutes, Andrew decided that the last statement needed some qualification. It wasn't far to Cheriton Shawe on the map. Doubts began to assail him. The conductor may have put him on the wrong track. Andrew decided to wait and question a pedestrian who was coming along some distance behind him. He waited, but the pedestrian turned off into a bypath that led to an area of glasshouses. He walked on. On one side, there were rows and rows of glasshouses. They had vegetables growing in them and seemed deserted.

At last a car appeared. He signalled, but the driver drove on, ignoring him. Another driver stopped.

"Cheriton Shawe?" he said. "Hop in."

He was a small man, dried up, gnome like. He drove slowly and grimly.

"What sort of place is Cheriton Shawe?" Andrew asked.

"I don't like the pub," the man answered after some thought.

"Know Walden House?"

"Never heard of it."

He did not seem to care for conversation. When there was some indication that Andrew might ask another question, he reached out and switched on the car radio. An orchestra was playing *Till Eulenspiegel*. He reached out again and hastily changed the station. A military band grappled with a waltz.

Andrew still heard *Till Eulenspiegel*. He swivelled to peer through the rear window. Absurd? Of course it was absurd. Especially as the whistler in the night had passed on his way, possibly innocent of any design but to reach his own home. And if you were inclined to argue that the Hallers and the Kretchmanns would be likely to pick up a fragment of Strauss, you had to remember that the trick was also within the scope of the Bert Smiths and the Alf Browns. Any time you turned the knob of a wireless set you might get *Till Eulenspiegel*. It didn't mean a thing in itself. To see anything significant in it, you had to be of a very suspicious turn of mind and perhaps a trifle neurotic.

Andrew looked back a second time.

"What's the matter?" asked the gnome. "Police after you?" "I'm interested in greenhouses."

"Wouldn't put my money in glass. It's too brittle. Here's your village. Don't say I didn't warn you against the pub."

Andrew used it merely to ask the way to Walden House. First to the left past the church, and you couldn't miss it; the big place on the rise with the high garden wall.

The wall was very high indeed and had a tiled coping. There were patches where it was mouldering away, but on the whole it was standing up to time and still efficiently obstructing the view of anyone who might be curious about the house and grounds.

Andrew skirted quite fifty yards of wall before he came to an opening. There were heavy brick gateposts. No doubt there had been ornamental gates, but now the only barrier to straying cattle was a length of rusty chain. The left-hand pier had been hit by a steam roller or something of equivalent weight.

The entry showed signs of having been churned into a morass by heavy traffic, but that had been some time ago; it was now grass covered. The drive, defined by deep ruts in neglected gravel, was visible for a few yards. Then it withdrew behind a dank screen of trees and overgrown shrubs. A notice board, newly painted, swung from the chain. It said: Private PROPERTY—No TRADESMEN.

Andrew stepped over the chain and, walking on the gravel between the ruts, started down the drive.

There was nothing round the first bend, only another screen of trees and bushes. Then the wheel ruts got impatient and, leaving the drive to its own graceful meanderings, crashed on through the undergrowth in a straight line. Andrew followed them and came upon a vista that pulled him up sharply. Beyond a wide, tree-dotted expanse of grass that may once have been a lawn stood a house.

It was unquestionably modern. The original idea, perhaps, had been to re-create a small French château, but even more lunatic counsels had prevailed and features reminiscent of a Norman castle and trimmings from a Rhenish Schloss had been applied with an apple-cheeked Teutonic exuberance that defied criticism. The whole looked like something from a beer-house frieze. There were corbels and machicolations everywhere. Cone-topped turrets sprouted from the corners. The main entrance had the stark simplicity of one of Ludovic of Bavaria's nightmares.

The house was not the only startling feature. The grassy area in front of it looked as if it were shared as storage space by a monumental mason and a medieval stonecutter. There were statues everywhere, and shaped building blocks of granite and sandstone. There were sections of fluted columns, bits of broken capitals, cornices and gargoyles strewn about as if Samson had been there brawling with the Philistines. But all this was as nothing compared with the staggering collection of statuary which cluttered the place. Venus rose from the sea of grass in a dozen different attitudes, Hercules flexed his muscles or bent a bow, Atlas stood braced under the weight of the world, Perseus flourished the head of Medusa, while dozens of nonentities looked on with blind-eyed approval.

Andrew found it impossible to believe that one frail girl with red hair could have accomplished all this work. She might be a most prolific sculptor, but she just could not have had the time in her short life. Was it possible, then, that she had acquired all this rubbish in order to study it at home? Then she must be mad, and mad without method. At least there was no detectable system in either the selection or the arrangement of it all. Tarnished metal pieces stood in close companionship with bits of marble, and strewn among them, peeping through trees and peering over bushes, were plaster casts of the more renowned classics. Inevitably the weather had made havoc. Rain had finally penetrated protective paint, sodden limbs had dropped off, weary feet of clay had given way, white bodies had fallen, and weeds had grown up to bury them. Chariot wheels had ground the dust of gods into the mire of Hertfordshire.

Chariot wheels or army truck tyres.

Andrew stepped forward cautiously. The Emperor Augustus stood up under a protecting oak, one arm flung out, looking as portentous and arresting as a traffic policeman. The arm had a sign fixed to it with wire, a piece of wood with faded letters in stencilled characters: TO THE LATRINES. An inscription in indelible pencil was easier to decipher:

> *Imperious Caesar, dead and turn'd to clay*
> *For alien legions -points the urgent way.*

A worn path through the trees was still only partially overgrown.

Andrew hastened to the front door and looked for a bell push. A note had been pinned to the wooden spike of a dummy portcullis. It said: *Gert, I've gone shopping. Hot up the pie and keep out of the studio.* It also said, by implication, that there was nobody in, that he would have to wait.

He tried the bell. It rang loudly, and that was all. He walked round the house, examining it in detail. The building was not so large as the perspective view had suggested, but it was still overpoweringly horrible. There were three floors with probably twenty to thirty rooms between them. It had an uninhabited look, but that may have been due to a prevalence of drawn blinds. A few windows on the top floor showed curtains. Perhaps the family was away somewhere. Perhaps Ruth Meriden had come home in advance of them.

A small patch of kitchen garden in the rear showed signs of cultivation, but nobody was at work in it. Andrew returned to the front of the house and browsed among the statues. The indelible pencil had been used quite extensively and not always by the same hand. Beards, moustaches and other adornments had been added to Olympian immortals and Roman heroes. One noble soldier, whose victories were won in the pre-Christian Era, wore upon his toga a badge of more recent design. The drawing, in most cases, was

76

extremely crude; but not nearly as crude as the comments and tags of mural wit that disfigured the flanks and other flattish surfaces of the female divinities.

Andrew wandered back to the house. He was just in time. The girl was approaching by a well-beaten short cut, wheeling a bike festooned with vegetables and paper parcels in string shopping bags. She was wearing a suede windbreaker, blue denim pedal-pushers, and tan sandals. Against the sombre background of fir and oak, her hair was a mop of incandescence.

She gave no sign of having seen him until she was about six feet away. Then she stopped.

"Hello! Looking for me?"

It was exactly the tone she had used at the airport—casual, indifferent, smug. Moreover, he had already opened his mouth to speak first and was thus left standing there gaping for a moment.

"Yes, Miss Meriden." Something about her called up severity in him. He opened his mouth to speak again.

"Well," she said, "I wasn't expecting you till next week."

This time he really gaped at her. She walked on past him.

"I've just got home," she added over her shoulder. "I'm afraid I haven't much to show you. Positively nothing of any account. No doubt they warned you. Seen my woman anywhere?"

He stumbled after her.

"No. I—"

"Late again. Come inside. I'll pop the pie in the oven; then I'll be with you."

Inside the hall a stencilled sign on the first door said: Q.M. STORES—*keep out.*

She called back from a bend in the corridor: "Wait upstairs. You'll find more light."

He found more tidiness, also. The ground floor was a wreck. The walls looked as if an elephant had been taking kicks at them. One floor board was up. Dry rot in others made walking perilous. But there were none of these hazards upstairs. The flooring was intact, and carpeted. The stencilling, too, was in a better state of preservation. Andrew passed BATTERY OFFICE and contemplated OFFICERS' MESS for a moment. Memory thus stimulated was a shade depressing, and he found no ease before a door marked BATTERY COMMANDER. He recalled one battery commander with septic tonsils. They had managed to get hold of a bottle of gin and . . .

The corridor was wide, with mullioned windows. It was like a small gallery and there were sculptures at intervals. There were a bust of a woman by Maillot, a girl's head by Epstein, a small Heracles by Bourdelle, an old man by Rodin. At least, the chiselling strongly suggested these masters, but he rejected the idea that they could be genuine. Copies, of course; student pieces, chipped out for the annual exhibition of the Hertford Society of Arts, and now proudly preserved by the young sculptor. Here it became quite obvious what that critic meant by her eclecticism. There wasn't an original line in any of the work. The Epstein, for instance, was pure Epstein. The Bourdelle departed from a characteristic devotion to plastic truth only in so far as it betrayed the smugness of the transcriber. The signature of Ruth Meriden was there to read. But it wasn't bad. Andrew knew enough about this sort of sculpture to realise that it wasn't bad. And, putting prejudice aside, looking at them fairly objectively, the other things weren't bad either.

She came up the staircase, observing him quizzically.

"Like the show?" she inquired.

He had to say something, but it really was embarrassing. He was suddenly conscious of a dreadful weakness in some of the work.

"Very good," he murmured. "Really quite good."

"Junk!" she said.

He was surprised at this modesty, but also resentful. After all, he had merely tried to be polite. Still. . .

"I wouldn't call it junk," he answered generously. "Some of it has feeling. The head of the archer is very good. Bourdelle himself might have done it."

"Bourdelle himself did do it," she retorted. "It's one of the early sketches for the big bronze in the Luxembourg. Poor old Emile! He never could get away from Rodin. Born fifty years later, he would have been a good sculptor. Let's go upstairs."

At that moment he would have liked the stairs to open and engulf him. It eased his embarrassment only a little to realise that she was unaware of what had been in his mind. She led the way to a long low attic with a considerable area of leaking skylight. She smiled as she opened the door. It was the first time he had ever seen her smile, and in that revolutionary moment he made an important discovery. There was nothing smug about her. She had not meant to be rude when she rejected his offer of help at the airport. She had been behaving merely in her normal casual manner. Through his absurd reaction to an imaginary snub, he had formed a wrong impression of her. The reality was that she was more trustful than suspicious. She accepted him now on completely even terms. She seemed to see him as a connoisseur who was interested in her work, and she, the artist, had invited him to view it. The accord was complete, and he hesitated to break it. The misconception, or whatever it was, afforded him an opportunity to study her. He would choose the moment to reveal himself.

The long room was fitted up like a carpenter's workshop. There were benches with all kinds of vices and wheels. There was a lathe and an electric saw. There were polishing and burnishing devices, and backing the main bench was a long rack of gleaming tools, including handsaws of all kinds.

She said: "I'm really very sorry, but I can't remember your name."

"Maclaren," he answered. "Andrew Maclaren."

"Maclaren," she repeated experimentally.

Along the wall opposite the benches and the lathe were a series of round, waist-high pedestals, each surmounted by an unusual object made of a plastic that looked like glass. The objects followed varied geometric patterns. None of them was very large. The tallest could not have measured much more than two feet from base to tip.

It was a fragile, pyramidal thing of bisecting planes.

"I'm beginning to remember," the girl said. "You're the man the Glasgow critic spoke to me about. I had your name mixed up. I thought it was Macartney."

He let that pass, making a noise in his throat that he hoped was noncommittal as well as inarticulate. He had no wish to impose on her, but this was definitely not the moment for revelation. She was looking on him as a human being. It was just as if she had removed a pair of sunglasses and he were seeing her eyes for the first time.

"This is the thing I'm working on." She picked up a large drawing from the bench and held it up for his inspection. It was another of those objects, but here projected in perspective on the two dimensional sheet. It was like a sea shell with a highly complex series of convolutions—except that it was nothing like a sea shell.

"Too intricate," she commented. "I'll try to simplify it when I get it under my fingers. There's a feeling here, I think." Her tool scarred right hand reached graspingly towards one corner of the drawing, then described arabesques in the air. "Something new. I'm sick of these' eternal comparisons. I must stand alone. Even the most incompetent critics must be made to see that I do stand alone."

"They talk such a lot of rot," Andrew murmured.

"Perhaps it's because they have to deal with such a lot of rot." Miss Meriden was grave. She lifted the drawing once more. "What do you see in this?"

He stared helplessly.

She went on. "I believe that this sort of art must create a new language. There may be here something that cannot be put into words, yet the thought is to be read by the sensitive mind. It must be inevitable, invariable, or the art is false. What does it give you?"

From gaping, he gulped. It gave him a complete blank.

"Nothing," he murmured reluctantly. "Unless you mean it's a sea—"

He was going to say sea shell, but it suddenly struck him that this would be one of the objectionable comparisons.

Again the imaginary spectacles came from the blue eyes.

"That's really remarkable," she said. "Nothingness, then the sea. Primordial. You feel it? This!" She pointed to some of the more excessive convolutions. "Before thought."

"Yes," he agreed uneasily. "Before thought."

She watched him with a gleam of appreciation in her eyes, then led him across the floor to one of the displayed objects. "This is one of the earlier studies," she told him. "To be disregarded, naturally. But I'd like your ideas."

It was a primitive form of harp in transparent plastic, if it was anything. On second thought it was three harps stuck together. Either that or a dimpled bottle with the dimples pressed in to a point of dissolution. The harp suggestion was conveyed by a series of white strings that seemed to be imbedded in the plastic. Whatever you might think of it as a construction, the craftsmanship was superb.

Ruth Meriden leaned forward and touched an electric switch. The pedestal began to revolve slowly. Shifting light on the turning surfaces of perspex made enchanting effects. This might not, in the ordinary sense, be sculpture, but Andrew was full of approval. The only thing he regretted was that it had to mean anything. It was acutely embarrassing to be asked to make something out of nothing. It was like expecting a magician to produce a rabbit when the poor man was obviously without his top hat.

"Well?" inquired Miss Meriden, impatient for the rabbit.

He had seen the word "Etude" on a label before the pedestal began to turn. It recalled again the criticism he had read; he fished in memory for a tag from it.

"Music," he answered her at last. "Scarlatti."

"No." The artist was disappointed. "Beethoven," she insisted. "Definitely Beethoven. Possibly the Waldstein Sonata."

She revolved the delicate pyramidal effect. Little pagodas turned within pagodas and glancing lights made chandeliers of ice. This time he had it. The Snow Queen's Palace.

"I call it Shive Dagon," Ruth Meriden announced. "Just as a joke, of course. It's really an abstraction. I've never been in Burma."

"I like it," Andrew asserted. "It has brio."

She looked at him with new attention, but this had nothing to do with his borrowed comment. She was puzzled. "Did you say your name was Maclaren?" she asked. "I can't get rid of the feeling that we've met somewhere before. It keeps growing on me. Were you at the Edinburgh Festival last year?"

"No." Andrew shook his head, but inwardly he nodded to himself. This was the moment. "I was on the plane from Athens the other day." It startled her, he thought. At any rate she was arrested in a movement and turned slightly to stare at him.

"Then you're not . . ." She broke off helplessly. Little coruscations from the revolving abstractions cast ripples of light between them.

"Of course," she said, making up her mind. "You're the man who spoke to me at the airport in Brussels. You . . ."

"I thought you needed help with the porter."

"It was kind of you." The belated acknowledgement came in a friendly tone. Then a suspicion took the warmth from her voice. "What are you doing here?"

"I had to see you. About Brussels. There was no time to write, so I came out on the chance."

She looked completely mystified. "Why should you want to"

"To warn you." It tumbled out as if that had been his sole purpose. "I wanted to reach you before the police."

"The police! What on earth are you talking about?"

"I was afraid you mightn't have heard," he said. "Kusitch is dead."

"Kusitch?" She frowned impatiently. "Let me get it clearly. Somebody named Kusitch is dead. Is that what you said?"

"Yes. He was taken from the Risler-Moircy. He was murdered. The Brussels police found his body in the Bois de la Cambre."

"Kusitch?"

"Yes. Shot through the head."

"And my name is Ruth Meriden? Is that right?"

"Let us be serious, Miss Meriden," he suggested. "This man was on the plane from Athens to Brussels. He had your address written down in a Green Line Coach Guide. Also he was carrying a review of your show at the Blandish Gallery."

"This address?" The girl seemed genuinely puzzled. "You mean he was coming here to see me? If he was that interested, why didn't he speak to me on the plane?" She shrugged helplessly. "I never heard of anyone named Kusitch. Am I supposed to have done so?"

"You may have known him by another name." "I knew no one on the plane. Did you say he was a Greek?"

"I said he joined the plane at Athens. He was from Yugoslavia, from Dubrovnik. And you've just come from Dubrovnik, haven't you?"

"Yes, I have. What about it?" Her voice rose. "What *is* all this?"

"That's what I want to find out, Miss Meriden. I came here in the hope that you might be able to tell *me.*"

She surveyed him coolly. Then she put her hand out and stopped the revolving pagoda.

"What exactly do you want, Mr. Maclaren?" she said curtly.

"*Doctor* Maclaren," he corrected her.

The absurdity of the correction was to occur to him later. At that moment it was important that she should find him a responsible person. The word "Doctor" always reassured displaced persons.

It did not reassure Miss Meriden. She looked faintly but not agreeably amused.

"Is that what the police call you?" she inquired.

Andrew stared at her. "The police?"

She nodded. "You must know the kind of thing," she said sweetly: "'John Smith, alias Andrew Maclaren, alias The Doctor. Poses as medical man or art critic. Works new version of old Spanish prisoner confidence trick using mysterious Yugoslav as bait.' How much are you after, Dr. Maclaren, and where do I send the money?"

For a moment he stared at her speechlessly. Then he exploded.

"Well, of all the confounded impertinence," he began.

She turned away contemptuously. "'Blusters when challenged,'" she added. "Have you any proofs of your identity? Of course you must have. False passport and false identity card all complete. Well now, Doctor—or should it be 'Doc'?—do you get out or do I call the police?"

For a space of about ten seconds he stood there silent. He was shaking with anger now and could feel the blood tingling away from his face. With an effort he brought his voice under control.

"I think you'd better call the police," he said. She glanced at him over her shoulder. "Aren't you taking things a little too far, Doc?"

He felt in his pocket. "I'm going to take them a great deal farther, Miss Meriden. As far as I'm concerned you can go to blazes' and stay there, but you're going to apologise to me first. Now then . . ." He put the contents of his breast pocket on the bench. "Passport and identity card, forged of course, but nice pieces of work. Then there's a document accrediting me to the International Red Cross organisation. Again forged. And there's this letter appointing me to the staff of the Kingsland Road Eye Hospital. That's a risky one, of course, because you can easily telephone the hospital and check on it. But the bluff usually works. Take a look, Miss Meriden."

She was watching him now. His eye met hers. Then she stepped forward and, picking up the papers, glanced through them quickly. He watched her vindictively. When she came to the letter she paused, then went back to the beginning of it and read again.

"Well?" he demanded.

Suddenly she began to laugh.

He stared at her angrily.

She went on laughing. "Oh dear, oh dear," she gasped, "my dear Dr. Maclaren, I do apologise, but really ..." A fresh paroxysm seized her. "I'm truly sorry," she managed at last, "but you must see how funny it is. . . . 'Blusters when challenged.' . . . Oh dear! I am so sorry. . . ."

And then Andrew began to laugh too.

After a bit it was arranged that he should stay to lunch.

Over the pie, which emerged eventually from the oven, he told her the story from the beginning. But when he paused expectantly at the point where the *Mary Isabella* came into it, she looked blank.

"I still don't see what all this has to do with me," she said. "Is the *Mary Isabella* important?"

"Well, it should be. It's a yawl-rigged fishing craft and your father bought it in Yugoslavia before the war."

"My father?"

"Isn't John Quayle Meriden your father?" She sighed wearily and without replying got up from the table.

"What's the matter? *Isn't* he your father?"

She gripped the back of a chair firmly. "My father," she said a trifle bitterly, "died when I was five. John Meriden was my uncle and my guardian."

"Was?"

"*He* died four months ago. I am his heiress."

"Oh."

She flung an arm out dramatically. "You see this house?"

"Yes, indeed."

"Mine. You saw that rubbish in the grounds?"

"It was difficult to miss."

"Mine." She sat down again somewhat violently and leaned across the remains of the pie. "Uncle John," she said venomously, "was what polite people call an eccentric. In fact, he was what the Americans call a jerk. He made his money betting on the Stock Exchange. He was on the lunatic fringe. He bought anything he thought looked like a bargain—anything worthless going cheap. Where near-idiots feared to tread, Uncle John clumped in with both feet. But when any near-idiot would have lost his shirt—if you can follow the metaphors—Uncle John, the full and complete idiot, hit the jackpot. Not once, but four times! He'd have soon lost the lot again, of course, in the ordinary way and serve the old fool right.

Unfortunately, he had an honest stockbroker to deal with and this idealist absolutely refused to handle any more of Uncle John's fancy business. He said it was silly. Either Uncle John put his fancy money in some decent securities or he could take his account elsewhere. In what must have been Uncle John's last moment of sanity, he agreed. But that was his last moment. From then on he became the world's number one bargain-hunting nitwit. Anything going cheap he bought. You see this house? A fleabite! There's stuff all over the world as far as I can see. Bargains! It was snuffboxes one week, anchors the next. A steam yacht, a 1922 Grand Prix racing car . . . do you know why I went to Yugoslavia?" "I was wondering that."

"He even bought a palace! A palace! I ask you! That's why I had to go. There's the Yugoslav Bureau of Alien Property mixed up in it. I had to go in person to agree to an inventory and sign papers. We'll end up by owing them money of course. You see, he collected lawsuits as well."

"What about fishing boats?"

"Wait a minute. I'm trying to think. Zavrana's the port near this ridiculous palace of his—of mine that is. Uncle John was at Zavrana with the yacht, *Moonlight*. *Moonlight! A* silly great tub of a thing that ran away with a fortune. If I wanted a few pounds for schooling, you'd have thought I was asking for the earth. But he spent enough on *Moonlight* in a week to educate an army. There wouldn't have been a penny left if the Admiralty hadn't requisitioned her during the war. Luckily she was sunk, so it may not be so bad in the end. Uncle John wouldn't settle for the compensation they offered, but I shall. At least I think so. Nobody knows yet whether the estate's bankrupt or solvent."

"Isn't there anyone who can help you?"

"There's Aunt Clara in Brussels."

"Is that the one who met you at the airport?"

"Yes, but she's nearly as dotty as Uncle John."

"What about *Mary Isabella?*"

"Oh yes. I'm sorry. I didn't mean to run on so. I've been thinking.

There was something about a boat. The Yugoslavs wanted to know if Uncle John had taken it to England with *Moonlight.*"

"And did he?"

"I don't know."

"Perhaps he did. Kusitch must have thought it was here if he'd come all the way here to look for it."

"But how do you know he was looking for it?" she asked.

"I'm guessing. Did your uncle never mention the boat at any time?"

She sighed. "He mentioned so many things. There might be a note about it in one of his diaries." "Diaries?"

It seemed that, characteristically, Uncle John had been an inveterate diarist. For years he had made it a habit to write down all the dullest happenings in his life from day to day. If he had ever heard of the craft again, he would surely have recorded the fact. The difficulty would be to comb through the books. There were quite a number of them.

"They're in the Battery Office downstairs," Ruth Meriden explained. "The gunners left some useful shelving. Shall we go down?"

The room was small and overcrowded. A pine folding table of a stark military pattern was straining under the weight of ceramics and more statuary. Great jars that looked like stage properties for the Forty Thieves stood on the floor, and there were a few broken chairs to complete the junk-shop effect. The shelving climbed all the way up one wall and it was piled with a varied collection of books in heavy bindings. Stacked against the other walls, or leaning here and there in solitary state, were great oil paintings in monstrous gilt frames. A portly figure in mayoral fur and chains of office stared challengingly across at another portly figure in a navy blue jacket and white yachting cap.

"Uncle John," Ruth Meriden explained.

"Both of them?"

"Both of them."

The man had a terrifying jauntiness, and an equally terrifying complacency. The twinkle in the eye and the cocksureness of the carriage told you that life must have been lots of fun for John Quayle Meriden, though the obstinate mouth and the idiot-blue eyes might make you doubt whether it had been quite so funny for the people who had had to deal with him. You could be sure, anyway, that he had exacted some devotion to his interests. He looked very well fed and cared for. Someone had polished up that chain of office till it shone. Someone had pressed those nautical slacks till they were fit for the commodore of any fleet. He was king baby with a teething ring suspended from his neck. He was mother's little sailor boy just before he was sick over his nice new uniform. He was egotism incarnate. He had been, as Miss Meriden had indicated, a jerk.

The diaries were readily distinguishable from the rest of the books. They were of a quarto shape issued annually by a firm of stationers, and quite uniform except for slight variations in binding style over the years. They stood together neatly and in chronological order. They went back to 1912, and reached forward to the current year.

It was a formidable collection, but Andrew could console himself with the thought that he would not have to go back beyond the start of the war in 1939 for possible references to the yawl.

"I haven't much spare time just now, but I'll help you as much as I can," Ruth Meriden said. "It's going to be quite a job, isn't it? You'd better take some of the books back to town with you."

This trustfulness, this confidence in him, was an agreeable development, but he had to admit it was offset by the hint that, now that the joke was over, he had better hurry about his business and leave her to her work. He made a pile of diaries, and she found a piece of string for him.

"If the police call on you," he said, "there'll be no need to tell them about the yawl. Unless they ask you specifically about the registration number."

"Why should we hold anything back?" she demanded.

He had no wish to discuss his motive, his disgust with Jordaens and his determination to teach the fellow a lesson.

"We ought to find out the meaning of the yawl," he asserted; "try to discover why Kusitch was so interested."

"I've been thinking," she said. "We might get some information from Captain Braithwaite. He used to be skipper of *Moonlight*. He lives at Thames Ditton these days."

He rose to it eagerly. "Is on the phone?"

"Yes, but I'm not. I had it cut off." She smiled enchantingly. "So you see I couldn't really have called the police. I'll come down to the village with you on your way home. We'll call him from the post office."

Here was another hint that she was bustling him off, but he had no cause for complaint. She was being helpful. She also jotted down his address and telephone number, in case she needed it. She looked at her watch. She knew the coach times by heart. He would be able to catch the three-sixteen. That would allow ample time for everything, if they started fairly soon. She walked him rapidly to the post office, got Captain Braithwaite on the telephone, then handed over the instrument. "You talk to him," she said.

The Skipper remembered the yawl quite clearly, and what he had to say confirmed the final details of Charley Botten's story. John Meriden had wanted the craft for use as a tender, but it had never been brought into commission. It had been drawn up on a slip at Zavrana and was undergoing repairs when John Meriden bought it. The repairs were still under way when the war broke out, and John Meriden had sailed away hastily in the *Moonlight,* abandoning the newly bought tender.

"Most likely the Italians grabbed it when they overran the coast," Captain Braithwaite said. "If so, they probably beat the insides out of it. In any case, it would cost more than it's worth to recover it. You tell Miss Meriden she'd better write it off. Personally, I wouldn't be surprised if it isn't at the bottom of the Adriatic."

"You don't think Mr. Meriden brought it back to England?"

"I'd be amazed if he did. Anyway, I wouldn't know. We had a quarrel on that voyage home, and I left him to do a job of work for the Navy. I never spoke to him again. I never wanted to. What are you, a lawyer of his?"

"No. A friend of Miss Meriden's. If her uncle had recovered the yawl, have you any idea where he would have moored it?"

"Son, you take a map and stick a pin in it. Left to that fellow, it might be among the houseboats of Srinagar or in the middle of the Gobi Desert. Tell Miss Meriden not to bother about it. It wouldn't be worth a Chinese dollar today. Ask her to speak to me."

Her contribution to the conversation seemed to be mainly laughter. He watched her face through the glass side of the booth. Most people looked quite ugly when they laughed. Oddly enough, she didn't.

"Not much help from the old boy," she commented when she emerged. "Perhaps we should take his advice and forget about the yawl."

Andrew shook his head. "We'll forget about it when we know it's at the bottom of the sea."

"You must be a good doctor," she said. "You never give up."

She walked a little way with him. She asked about his work, and they talked of Greece. The trip to Yugoslavia, she said, had offered her the opportunity to see Greece, otherwise she would have stayed at home.

They parted at the turn into Wyminden Lane, and now she impressed on him that he must hurry. He hurried. He looked back and saw her going down the road to Cheriton Shawe. When he looked back a second time she had disappeared. A sudden discontent seized him; but it was a sweet discontent. He hurried.

On the coach to London, he opened one of the diaries and began to read:

Resigned from board of P.H. & D.B.—Gave C.H. a piece of my mind.—Not satisfied with Ruth's school report; money not justified. Fear she is complete blockhead.

He did not go on with the reading. His mind was full of the blockhead. He saw her as he had seen her going back to Cheriton Shawe with the sun in her hair. The image was still with him when he reached home and opened the door of his borrowed flat. It was several seconds before he realised the change in the place. Then his heart gave a bump and he stubbed the toe of one shoe against the rug as he moved forward into the room.

Papers were strewn on the floor, desk drawers turned out, cupboards ransacked. There was the same state of disorder in the bedroom.

As the first sense of shock subsided, he began to think. There had been nothing here, nothing that any sane burglar would want, nothing of any conceivable consequence except the notes Charley Botten had made about the yawl.

He felt hastily in his pockets. Then he remembered that he had tucked the slip of paper away in a pocket. Jacket? No. He had been wearing his dressing gown.

The garment had been cast down on the floor by the intruder. Andrew picked it up and searched in the pockets. The slip of paper had gone.

Eight

For a moment or two the loss seemed a calamity, then Andrew came to his senses. The page from the telephone pad merely recorded certain facts about the fishing craft. For the whereabouts of the craft, if that was what the thieves wanted, they might just as well have followed Captain Braithwaite's advice and stuck a pin in a map.

The first shock having given way to a feeling of murderous annoyance, Andrew made a careful examination. It was easy to see how the flat had been entered. Anyone who watched for an opportunity could walk into the building unobserved, as the front door was invariably left open during the day. Once the upper landing was gained, the problem presented little difficulty to the intruder. He had merely to split off a section of the doorjamb by the lock and force back the latch with a pliable blade.

As Andrew proceeded, methodically replacing scattered papers and restoring drawers to furniture, he was confirmed in his immediate impression that this was no mere sneak-thief affair. Lang's property included a few pieces of silver that would have been worth something to the ordinary burglar, but these had been ignored. Again and again Andrew went over the contents of the flat, checking his own things, checking Lang's as far as he could, and he was confident in the end that the scrap of paper from the pocket of his dressing gown was the only thing missing.

So much for the fatuous self-confidence of Inspector Jordaens, to say nothing of the imbecile Stock. He had thrown the clue of the SS 729 in their faces, and they had tossed it back at him. It was true he had not at that time known about its relation to the yawl, but he had insisted on its importance. Now he was vindicated, and by the enemy! Possibly by Kretchmann and Haller, the Inspector's own pet suspects.

The sense of vindication had no soothing effect on Andrew. He picked up the telephone and dialled Scotland Yard. Now he would really talk to that nitwit Stock. He would demand action, protection, compensation, everything.

First of all he had to demand Detective-Sergeant Stock. There was a delay. He was asked politely to state his business. He said his business was with Detective-Sergeant Stock.

"I'm sorry, sir. Detective-Sergeant Stock is not available. Who is calling him?"

"It doesn't matter who's calling. I want to speak to him personally."

"He's not on hand, sir. Will you leave a message?"

"No, I will not leave a message!"

He slammed the receiver down hard. He paced the still untidy flat, his mind erupting. The police! What was the good of the police? When you wanted them, they were never available.

It was quite a few minutes before he got round to the thought that he should have left the telephone number for Stock. Or he should have asked where he could get in touch with Jordaens, if the fellow were still in England. He took another turn or two before he started for the telephone again. Then, as he reached out a hand, the instrument exploded into ringing noise.

Scotland Yard! They had traced his call! Or wasn't that possible with the automatic exchanges?

"Hello!" he said angrily.

"Hello! Is Dr. Maclaren there?"

His heart jumped as he recognised the voice. "Dr. Maclaren speaking," he said weakly.

The voice said: "This is Ruth Meriden. I didn't recognise your voice. You were shouting. I just thought you might like to know that I have been visited by the police."

"Oh!" He was still recovering.

"You don't seem very interested. Anyway, it was nothing. Just routine questions. When I said I had never met Kusitch, that was almost the end of it. There was nothing about the yawl."

"I didn't think there would be. Was the fellow a Belgian, named Jordaens?"

"No. He was from Scotland Yard. Quite a pleasant person. Not at all the sort you led me to expect."

"Not Detective-Sergeant Stock?"

"Yes. That was the name."

"Oh!"

He thought he would tell her about his burglar, but hesitated. It might alarm her. He must consider it first.

"You sound odd," she said. "Has anything happened?"

"Nothing of consequence." He had a sudden wish to see her again, a wish that made everything else appear trivial. "May I run out tomorrow?" he asked her.

"If it's anything important, you'd better tell me now," she answered. "Tomorrow is impossible for me. I'm going to be busy. I have to call at the Blandish Gallery in the morning."

"What about lunch?"

"No good, I'm afraid."

"Oh! Well... let me know if you find anything in the diaries."

"Of course. I must be off now. Good-bye."

"Good-bye."

It sounded inane to him even while the words were being said. He put the telephone down slowly. He held it for a moment on the cradle, then snatched it up quickly, moved by sudden fear.

"Hello!" he called. "Hello! Hello!"

He was too late. There was just a dialling tone. He replaced the instrument again and reasoned against his anxiety. It was absurd.

She could be in no danger. The fact that his flat had been entered that afternoon was almost an assurance of her safety. No one had followed him to the country. The shadow had been otherwise engaged, and had secured what he had been after all along, the registration number of the yawl. Even if the man deduced from the gibberish of Charley Botten that the yawl was the property of John Quayle Meriden, there was nothing to lead him to Walden House. The only possible contact with her was through Botten's friends, the Pascoes in Falmouth; and the Pascoes were unlikely to give the address to a stranger. It was certain that, too, Kusitch had not helped them much; otherwise his murderers would have gone straight for their objective, instead of chasing after a harmless doctor.

So the girl was safe. . . .

He looked at his watch. He wanted to confirm his reasoning. He called up Charley Botten, but got no response.

The second time he called up, Charley gave him his confirmation. He had tried every available source for Meriden's address before telephoning to Falmouth.

"Do me a favour, Charley," Andrew urged. "Phone Pascoe again and ask him to see that the address is given to nobody; not even to Scotland Yard."

"What the devil are you up to?" Charley demanded.

"Sticking my long neck out, only it isn't so long." He tried to speak lightly but in his own ears sounded merely feeble. "Will you make that call to Falmouth at my expense?"

"I will if you'll tell me what you're doing."

"Not tonight. I'm busy."

Andrew went to a restaurant in the neighbourhood for an early dinner. His purpose was less to get a meal than to find out if he were still being followed. Before he reached the restaurant he was reasonably certain that there was no one on his trail. Going home, he took a circuitous route and made elaborate tests. The result was negative. He felt quite pleased with himself when he bolted the door of his flat. He was no longer being watched, and the enemy had got virtually nothing for his pains. At this moment of satisfaction, he decided against a second effort to report the burglary to Stock. He could not give up this important evening to the further entertainment of Inspector Jordaens and his taciturn yes-man. He had far too much to do.

He proceeded to do it. He sat in Lang's armchair with tobacco, cigarettes, and the Meriden diaries on the table beside him. The books he had brought from Walden Hall covered the years from 1944 onward. Ruth Meriden had promised to examine the diaries from '39 to '43, but he believed he had selected the more promising period. The yawl must have been recovered after the war, if it had been recovered at all, but he began with the year '44 and read steadily for two hours, taking up one book after another. He made coffee, rested a while, then returned to the job.

The diaries were the dull, stupid reflections of a dull, stupid man. John Quayle Meriden had loved John Quayle Meriden dearly; and in this passionate affair there had been room for no other person. He had been absorbed completely by everything about himself. His purchases, his collections, his hates, his petty vengeances, what he said to a careless servant, even the state of his digestive tract, everything was recorded with remorseless attention to detail. And throughout it all, recurring like an hallelujah, was the John Q. Meriden word of praise and triumph—"cheap."

"Bought copy of the Canova Venus cheap. . . . Am offered two genuine Copleys cheap. . . . Got onto Pierce-Arrow in good condition cheap. . . . Mill and cottage cheap . . . brasswork cheap . . . cheap . . . cheap . . . cheap . . ."

Ruth Meriden was a constant cause of displeasure. The school reports were never good enough, the fees were always too high. It was a sheer waste of money, because the girl, like her useless mother, had nothing in her. No culture. No talent. Give her domestic training and marry her off. Get rid of her.

Yet there had been quite a storm when Ruth had insisted on going to Aunt Clara in Belgium in the second year after the war's end. Why couldn't she finish her education in England? And, anyway, a girl of eighteen should be thinking of settling down, acquiring some sense of responsibility, preparing for the great fortune she would inherit.

That was curious, and there was to be more of it. It went on as if John Quayle Meriden had suddenly taken a new view of himself. He was now the devoted guardian whose one aim had been to accumulate a store of wonderful things, of money and property, for the girl. And his reward was that she must go gadding about in Europe with the detestable Aunt Clara.

Then sculpture! More expensive lessons. Not worth the money. The girl had no idea of art, making tinkling toys out of wire and bits of brass. And this, after all the trouble he had taken to surround her with the great works of the Masters. If she wanted sculpture, let her look in the garden at Cheriton Shawe.

He had grandiose plans for the restoration of Walden Hall, as soon as an ungrateful government had settled up with him. He would build a new wing, make a pleasure garden of fountains and statuary. He would show her!

Andrew paused before he turned the page. Overleaf there was only one entry, and that at the end of the week.

"It is terrible here without Ruth. Why doesn't she come home?"

But that was an isolated phenomenon. For the other three hundred and sixty-four days of the year, the incredible possibility that self-love might not be all was quite discounted.

The diary for the next day went on as usual. John Q. was right back on form, sacking servants, vilifying acquaintances, starting lawsuits, buying things cheap.

Andrew stopped reading. He wanted to think about Ruth Meriden, to see her against this monstrous background. It was important to him. It was far more important than any search for a lost fishing craft. For the background threw the girl into relief, and the more he learned of it, the more she stepped out in front of it, detached, disowning it, insisting upon her own identity. She was a good person.

Perhaps there had been moments when John Quayle Meriden might have been pitied, but it was difficult to make any allowances when you remembered those heroic, badly painted canvases of the mayor and the yachtsman. One should go no further than to say that, as a psychological study, he was mildly interesting.

The girl was very interesting, and not as a psychological study. He saw her as she went down the road to Cheriton Shawe, waving a friendly hand.

He closed his eyes and the haze of contemplation thickened into darkness. He awoke with a start when the diary slipped from his knee and hit the carpet.

It was very late, but there wasn't much left of the year 1948. He was determined to finish it off before he went to bed.

He found his lost place with some difficulty and read on. Meriden had devoted '48 to tracing and retrieving property in the war torn countries, and the diary was full of incomprehensible details with a free use of abbreviations and meaningless initials.

Andrew thought he would have to give it up after all. He was too sleepy; couldn't keep alert enough. Blinking, he turned a page. Then his eyes came wide open and he jerked up in his chair. It was there at last, in the first entry on the new page.

> *F. reports tender to Moonlight found at Bova Marina. Last heard from Dubrovnik it was missing, believed sunk. How the devil did it get from Zavrana to Calabria? Asking F. send full details.*

There was another entry five days later:

> *Heard from F. in Naples. Says escaping Italians seized tender at Zavrana and sailed it to Calabria where made "present" of it to fisherman. Present indeed! Instructing F.*

insist on return of my property, take up with Italian authorities and British representatives if necessary. Compensation?

Meriden had been interested. It seemed that he had had enough imagination to appreciate this extraordinary case of his tender to the lost *Moonlight*. He recorded every detail he could gather, and the odd bits of information that reached him over the next month told the full story.

Five deserters from the Italian Army of Occupation along the Dalmatian coast had made for Zavrana, had seized the yawl, had stolen provisions, and slipped from the port at night without difficulty.

Luck had sailed with them, for no patrol boat of any navy challenged them, and they had reached their objective, a lonely spot along the toe of Italy. They had found help there. The father of one of them was a Calabrian fisherman. The deserters had taken to the fastnesses of the Aspromonte, and vanished. The old fisherman had appropriated the yawl after securing false papers and distributing a few bribes. He had claimed to have acquired the craft in Reggio, from a Sardinian who had bought it in Corsica.

This involved invention had caused Meriden's agent some trouble, but finally he had taken a firm line with the fisherman. The old man had had no resources to meet a threat of proceedings from an Englishman with all the evidence of ownership. He had changed his tune and claimed salvage. He had found a derelict, drifting helplessly on a stormy sea towards the savage shore. At the risk of his life he had saved it. He had looked after it, kept it in order, painted it in bright colours twice a year. Fifty thousand lire would scarcely compensate him for the trouble and expense he had been to. It was true he had used the craft now and then, but merely to give the engine a run and to maintain the sails in good repair.

The sails were shreds and patches, no paintbrush had touched the yawl, it had been worked continuously, but the hull was sound

ERIC AMBLER

and the engine still running. The old boy had loved engines more than anything in the world. He had claimed to have been devoted to this one.

Meriden had been unmoved. Rather than pay one penny of ransom, he would see the tender at the bottom of the Mediterranean. He had issued a final warning. Then he had changed his mind and made a concession. On the last day of the year he had written: *Tired of F.'s arguments. Have agreed to pay Calabrian bandit £5. Sending E.J. to pick up tender and bring home. Not worth the expense, but E. pestering me for job with sick wife. Very dissatisfied with F. Anyone would think had no right to my own property. Pity Moonlight gone. Tender would have been useful. Get E. repair landing stage mill if draught all right for depth. Don't want to dredge. Can't waste more money over old tub unless survey proves her bargain.*

That was all. Andrew looked closely through the first three months of the next year's diary, but found no further reference to the yawl; nothing to indicate whether E.J. had picked her up at Bova Marina, no jubilant note of homecoming. The tender had dropped right out of the consciousness of John Quayle Meriden. Possibly the survey had proved her no bargain. In any case, Mr. Meriden had been busy with other affairs, writing to the War Office about damage done to Walden House, fighting with his lawyers over the extent of his claims, threatening to put the government out of office unless he were paid right down to the last penny. Only at the end of March was there an item that might be related, not to the yawl, but to the last entry about the yawl. It said:

> *E.J. pestering me again. Am sick of that whining Norski. Now wants to take his sick wife to Algiers. Says he can get a job there. Told him he won't get another penny out of me.*

In the interval E.J. may have made the trip to Calabria. Most likely he had, since the hunt for the craft had focused on England.

100

All the rest was surmise.

If it was safe to come to any conclusion, it was that Meriden had placed no special value on the yawl. If the craft contained a treasured object—something to start a chase across Europe and cause a murder in Brussels—Meriden could not have known about it, or he would never have haggled over the few pounds that fifty thousand lire represented at the time of the Calabrian's demand. Yet the lure for Kusitch and the others must have been placed in the yawl while she was at Zavrana or in Dalmatian waters, or Kusitch would not have known of it.

War loot? That's what it looked like. Kusitch was the expert, employed by his government, devoting all his time to the tracing of war loot. The trail of some stolen object had led to the yawl, and it was to be assumed that the object had remained on board through all the vicissitudes endured by the little craft.

It was a difficult assumption. The yawl had been repaired, launched again by some local authority, used in the port and nearby waters; it had been stolen by the Italian fugitives, sailed to Bova Marina, used by the old fisherman, and, possibly, brought back to England as the property of Meriden. An object would have to be pretty small to remain hidden under those circumstances.

Perhaps it had not remained hidden. Yet Kusitch had been so certain that he had staked his future on it; others had been so sure that they had used the desperate expedient of abduction from a hotel and followed it up with murder. The motive must be material gain, though it could be the suppression of a menace, the destruction of documents that threatened newly achieved careers. Treacheries, betrayals, treasons had smeared Europe in the wake of the Nazis. Men who had compromised themselves were anxious to forget; more anxious that others should never know about it. Documents stolen from archives could bring ruin. Documents could be safely hidden in a small craft and recovered later on for purposes of blackmail.

Meriden himself? Somehow it did not seem likely.

Andrew jotted down facts from the diaries on a sheet of note paper. He considered again and again the last entry about the tender. *"Get E. repair landing stage mill if draught all right for depth. Don't want to dredge."*

The meaning was clear enough. Meriden had meant to bring the yawl to a landing stage near some mill if the water was deep enough without dredging. Since he could order repairs to the landing stage he must own the property. There had been some reference somewhere to a mill and cottage, with the commendation "cheap" attached to it. A mill suggested a river, or at least a creek somewhere.

"Somewhere" was a wide word, but unquestionably a way had to be found to that mill.

Andrew frowned over his notes. Miss Ruth Meriden might be a very busy girl tomorrow, but she was going to see him sometime during the day.

Nine

HE WENT to bed with a feeling of satisfaction. His rest was well earned. The next day would be fruitful. In the dark he stretched out comfortably and thought, in the manner of John Quayle Meriden, of the coming discomfiture of Jordaens and Stock. He thought of it for quite a while before he fell asleep. He awoke suddenly in the night, disturbed by some troubled dream. In this half-waking state he believed he had heard a stifled shout, a cry. Kusitch again. He wished the fellow were not so restless. They had to be up early enough to catch the plane in the morning. Kusitch . . .

Reality returned with a rush. This was not Brussels. It was London, Lang's flat.

He got out of bed, quietly, and stood in the dark, listening. He heard sounds, the secretive sounds of someone creeping along the landing outside the flat. He remembered he had bolted the door, so that was all right. It could not be opened any longer as it had been during the day. He was safe. He had time to raise an alarm. They couldn't carry him off as they had carried off Kusitch.

The sounds continued, faint as the gnawing of mice. Then a stair creaked loudly. And another stair. The noctambulist had passed the landing and was creeping up the next flight, a home going tenant, thoughtful for his neighbours, anxious to disturb nobody.

That was all right. Go to bed again. Get more sleep.

But it was not all right. Fear had come up the stairs and entered the flat, bringing the thought of the girl in the lonely house at Cheriton Shawe.

He was at once desperately anxious and paralysed by the feeling that it was too late to help her. The argument that the enemy could not discover the link between John Quayle Meriden and Walden House now seemed absurd. Kretchmann and Haller were resourceful and ruthless. They had ruthless followers to help them: the shadow in Brussels, the whistler in London.

Andrew felt the prickle of sweat on his scalp.

One of them might have followed him to Cheriton Shawe while another stayed in London to search the flat. If he had been followed, then the lead would be obvious to them.

They would have gone to Walden House tonight. They would have questioned the girl, tortured her, demanding the whereabouts of the yawl. They would have refused to accept her plea of ignorance, and in their incredulity lay the danger for her. They were desperate men; would stop at nothing. Jordaens had been emphatic on that score. Deserters, gangsters, outlaws, murderers . . .

Were they also clairvoyants?

Andrew grasped at that question as a defence. He switched on the light and that, too, seemed to help. The thing was not to be believed. It was a night thought out of a bad dream. The Green Line coach had dropped him into solitude. The next stop was some distance on, and if anyone wanted to get off he had to wait for it. A shadow could not have come back all that way and picked up the trail. Wyminden Lane had been a desolation of glasshouses, and the one solitary pedestrian had turned off into that desolation, never to be seen again.

He had encountered no one else except the gnome who had given him a lift. Was it possible that the fellow had followed the coach from London in his car, had waited a reasonable time before overtaking him on Wyminden Lane so as not to rouse suspicion? A good way to find out the destination of a person was to offer him a lift. It was true that the gnome had asked no questions; had shown no wish to converse, but had not his need to do so been obviated by his passenger's naive inquiry about Walden House?

Andrew flinched at the thought of it. Then he remembered how quickly the gnome had changed the station on the car radio, cutting off *Till Eulenspiegel*. Andrew flinched again, but checked his racing thoughts. Could it possibly be maintained that such an act was significant of anything more than a dislike of tone poems and a preference for military bands?

Absurd! The fact was plain: the car could not have trailed him from London. It could not have picked him up outside the flat. He had taken the underground to Oxford Circus, and cars cannot follow you when you travel by tube.

He felt a little better, but still uneasy. He looked at his watch: four-thirty. It would soon be daylight. He would normally have slept till seven, but he knew it was no use going back to bed. The anxiety would keep on nagging at him, urging him to some unspecified act.

There was nothing rational to do except make coffee. He put on his gown and started the percolator. He sat down with the diaries again, and read on from where he had left off. He read and sipped coffee. There was no further reference to Calabria, the yawl, or the landing stage by the mill. But every time he encountered Ruth Meriden's name the nagging increased.

He would never forgive himself if any harm had come to her.

At the same time he assured himself that nothing could have happened. There was no question in his mind; there was merely the nervous demand for confirmation of what reason told him must be. Confirmation? He had only to find a car or a taxi to run him out to Cheriton Shawe. He might even hire a car to drive himself, for he had kept on renewing his licence, during his service abroad.

His watch told him it was too late. He had been too long over the diaries and coffee. By the time he dressed and got out to Walden House, she might be on the way to town, and then he would miss her altogether.

105

He bathed, dressed, breakfasted, and at nine o'clock reached the Blandish Gallery. The beautiful door of burnished bronze was locked. The hand-lettered placard in the bronze frame indicated that the exhibition was open from ten till five-thirty. The small Dufy was still in the large window. Its gaiety irritated him. It was of a world of sun and bright colour.

Andrew went away. When he returned some time before ten, the door was open. A decorative young lady was sympathetic, but not very informative. She had no idea when they would see Miss Meriden again, although there was some talk of another exhibition. His best course was to write to Miss Meriden and the Blandish Gallery would forward the letter.

"Look here," he said firmly. "Miss Meriden is coming in this morning. She told me so last night. I have to see her. It's most important, urgent. It's too late to catch her at Cheriton Shawe."

The girl was impressed. "It must be Mr. Hinckleigh," she said. "I'll look in his engagement book." She came back. "Perhaps you'd better wait for Mr. Hinckleigh."

"What time is the appointment?" he demanded.

"Ten-thirty," she admitted reluctantly. "Would you like to take a seat?"

He declined with thanks. He walked up and down the pavement outside. There was a man on the opposite side who looked like someone he had seen in the tube from Holland Park that morning, but he was wary of that sort of idea now. Once you had been followed, it was too easy to imagine that the attention was being repeated. He had satisfied himself last night that he was no longer under observation.

The man opposite entered a tobacconist's shop. He was inside for some time. Then he went briskly along the street and disappeared into a small arcade of shops. A tall man in a cap and an overlong grey raincoat that flapped about and slapped at his legs as he walked. Very different from that fellow in Brussels; not the remotest resemblance to old Jolly-Face of Holland Park.

Andrew checked himself for the second time in less than two minutes. It was idiotic to suppose that the whole world was interested in his movements. Even if the man had travelled by the Central Line, what was there to prove that he had not got on at Ealing Broadway?

A dark, slender person in a faultlessly cut tweed overcoat pushed at the bronze door of the gallery with a gloved hand that held a ball-top cane. Mr. Hinckleigh?

Andrew became uneasy again about Ruth Meriden. It was nearly half past ten, and, even while he looked along the street for her and watched the approach of every taxi, he was convinced that she would not come. All the fears of the night were on him again, and growing with every minute. He turned restlessly, looking up and down the street, and no longer glanced in the direction of the arcade.

Fool, he was! He should have rushed out to Cheriton Shawe when the thought first struck him. Or he should have called up Stock at Scotland Yard. There might have been time then, but now . . .

She was crossing the roadway, punctual to the minute.

He felt such a lift of relief, he could think of nothing to say to her. He stammered over words that were absurdly formal.

"Oh dear," she said, "I meant it when I said I had a busy day ahead of me. Is it really very important, Dr. Maclaren?"

She was looking very chic in a tweed suit and a minute hat.

"I'm glad you're all right," he said.

"You sound most anxious. Why shouldn't I be all right?"

"Well, of course ... I had to come along. I hope you don't mind. I found a lot about the yawl in the diaries."

"Oh, that yawl! I wonder if you're not taking it too seriously. Have you found out where it is?"

He told her what he had found out. Her interest seemed more polite than real, as if she had been merely humouring him. There was a change in her. Town, or the proximity of the Blandish Gallery!

She was now very much Brussels airport in her manner.

"We can't stand out here on the pavement all day," she said. "Let's go inside." Inside there were only the two of them and the water colours of Christophe Chambord. The long room, unlighted, dwindled away from the show window into the dimness of back premises.

Andrew produced the notes he had made from the diaries, and read them over quickly, from the first report of the agent F. about the finding of the yawl in Calabria to the references to E.J. and the repair of the landing stage.

Miss Meriden thought the F. referred to an Italian lawyer named Ferrani. She was quite certain that E.J. could be none but Ernest Jansen, formerly carpenter and mechanic in the *Moonlight* and latterly an old man of the sea on Meriden's back. It seemed Ernest had been the one retainer who could wheedle what he wanted out of his master. He might have been able to tell where the yawl was lying, but he had in fact taken his wife to Algiers and Ruth Meriden had no idea of how to get in touch with him. By now he was probably in Mauritius or Tristan da Cunha.

"What about the mill and this landing stage?" Andrew asked urgently.

"I really don't know," the girl told him. "I never heard of anything of the sort, but that doesn't mean that there mightn't be a whole collection of mills somewhere."

"And all your property. Surely the lawyers must know if there's a mill. It sounds a likely place: stream, water wheel, landing stage."

"I don't know. I'll have to—"

She turned at a sound of footsteps. The dark, slender person who had arrived in the beautiful tweed overcoat came quickly from the back premises. He was immaculate in Oxford grey. Behind him the decorative young lady paused to press switches, as if to give him an adequate lighting effect, but possibly she had just remembered Mr. Chambord's water colours.

The immaculate Mr. Hinckleigh swooped down.

"Ruth darling, why didn't you come through to the office?" he demanded. "I had no idea you were here. How is the new conception working out?" "Not too well, Percy." She seemed happy to see him, and that was something beyond comprehension to Andrew. "I'm having trouble with the inward planes," she added.

"My poor darling," said Mr. Hinckleigh perfunctorily. "I don't have to tell you how I feel for you, but I have complete confidence. Everything will work out. The important thing now is Alec Foster. The plan has been changed. He is not coming here. We are going to see him."

"Well, let me introduce Dr. Maclaren. This is Mr. Hinckleigh, Dr. Maclaren."

Andrew was short in response, but Mr. Hinckleigh was shorter. He nodded vaguely and turned back to the girl.

"Now, darling, we've no time to spare. I want you to glance at the letters we've exchanged, then we'll dash round the corner to the hotel. Foster's most impatient to meet you. If he can arrange his appointments, he wants to go out to Cheriton Shawe with us this afternoon. Now come along to the office, darling. We don't want to keep the great man waiting."

He hurried her off with an arm round her waist. Halfway down the avenue of water colours, he swung his head round and shot an "excuse me" at Andrew, but Ruth darling had not even this much grace. Andrew glowered. She had, it was true, given him a "look" before yielding to the caressing guidance of Mr. Hinckleigh. It was, in a way, an acknowledgement that he still existed; otherwise it might have been interpreted as an imperious order to wait.

Andrew waited. He had spent a sleepless night worrying about this girl; he had been up in the bright morning, trudging the street, waiting for her. And now, Percy Hinckleigh! He might have known it. When he cast his mind back to the reception room at the Brussels airport, he could almost say he had known it.

He was angry. He was sad and depressed. He was as depressed as if all the future had suddenly clouded over. There was nothing ahead, nothing but glaucoma and xerophthalmia and operations for the relief of intraocular pressure, and these things no longer interested him. He had wanted to spend the rest of his life tracking down yawls and confuting Belgian detective-inspectors, all with the ardent co-operation of red-haired girls, or, to put it bluntly, Miss Ruth Meriden. Perhaps he needed an operation himself, for the correction of cockeyed vision. Or a good healthy whack over the head to bring him to his senses. This business of murdered Yugoslavs and hidden yawls and insolvent heiresses had nothing to do with him. There was still time to walk out on it. Now. This minute. None of the others cared a brass farthing about it. Ruth Meriden, absorbed in her work, was completely indifferent. Why, then, should he care?

The decorative young lady was at his elbow, offering him a piece of paper.

"Would you like a catalogue?"

"No," he answered sadly. "No, thank you."

He turned and gazed out into the melancholy street over the top of the draped curtain that separated the window from the rest of the gallery. A man had halted on the pavement to peer in at the small Dufy: the tall man in the cap and the overlong grey raincoat who had recently gone into the arcade on the opposite side of the street.

Andrew started, drew back, then looked again, cautiously. The man was staring at the Dufy as if he wanted to hypnotise it. Dark eyes seemed deep-set under the peak of the cap, a thin nose projected, the lower part of the face had an effect of hard immobility as if it had been carved by a bad hand. There was an odd, animal sharp familiarity about the features, but the fellow was a type, of course. That was it: a type!

The singular deadness of the face was relieved only by the eyes. They were like currants. The man hated that little picture by Dufy. He stood in front of it for more than a minute, then he moved off in the direction of Oxford Street, a brown paper parcel tucked under one arm, the overlong raincoat flapping above his trouser cuffs.

Mentally Andrew shrugged. The fellow had done his shopping in the arcade, had taken a look at the painting, and passed on. Now there was a stout man examining the Dufy through a monocle, and he gave place to a lean youth in a blue denim boiler suit. One might as well suspect all as suspect one, and the absurdity of that was only too manifest.

Ruth Meriden touched his elbow. "I'm sorry I have to go off," she said. "This American dealer is most important. I'll see the lawyers and find out about the mill as soon as I can. I may be able to arrange it tomorrow. I don't know. I'll phone you when I get the information."

"All right," he said, with an attempt at indifference. "I've been thinking too. Perhaps we are taking it all too seriously."

She focused a curiously sharp look on him. She hesitated about what she was going to say. Then she obviously said something else.

"Well," she said, "we'll see."

Mr. Hinckleigh, coated again and with gloves and cane, was holding open the bronze door. On the pavement, the girl said: "We're going this way, Dr. Maclaren. Are you coming with us?"

"No. I go the other way."

He was not sure whither it led. He turned one corner and another, and perhaps two more. Corners were of no account. He was without a destination. He might have been a blind man tapping along for all he saw of the streets he traversed. His bitter preoccupation with Ruth Meriden left no chink for another thought, and it was only through her that he again approached the outside world. He had dismissed anxiety in his relief at seeing her. Now it wormed a way into his mind again, but he resisted it, bitterly now. He had been harried by groundless fears in the night. Were they any less groundless this morning? He looked about him and found he was in Oxford Street, approaching Marble Arch. He had nothing to do at Marble Arch, so he decided on the opposite direction.

Turning, he remembered the tall man in the flapping raincoat, and kept a lookout for him. As he walked on, that long grey coat became a symbol for him. It was, in absence, the groundless fear. If he encountered it again, then the fear would be real. He was confident, very confident, and it was not through the glaucoma of wishful thinking that he failed to see the coat. He went through the old tricks to prove it to himself. He invented new ones. He tried side streets and unpeopled back ways. He explored the mews and mazes of Mayfair. He dawdled over small purchases in obscure shops. No one followed him, yet he no longer found comfort in this certainty. He was too distracted about the mere existence of Miss Meriden to find comfort.

The walking had left him rather tired. He found a restaurant and lunched. When he was out in the street again, he thought of going home, but could not face an afternoon alone in the flat. Next he thought of looking up some of his neglected friends, but this idea had even less appeal for him.

He passed a cinema, hesitated, turned back and bought a ticket. There was a comedy that reminded him of the tall man's coat. It was much too long and it flapped badly; also it was very unfunny. He waited for the second film, and that wasn't funny either. It was about a young girl who lived with a strange family in a lonely country house full of long dark passages, winding staircases, and terrifying furniture. There were three brothers, an elderly housekeeper, and something that lived at the top of the house. One of the brothers was murdered, and then a hand came out of the darkness, seized the girl, and drew her behind a heavy curtain.

Andrew didn't wait for any more. He could not leave Ruth Meriden alone in that isolated house; he must insist that she stay in town till there was no longer any danger. If she objected, he would go to Stock or to someone else at Scotland Yard and insist that she be given protection.

The time was nearly four when he left the cinema. Possibly she would still be entertaining the American dealer and Mr. Hinckleigh at Walden House, but, if luck favoured him, the guests would be gone by the time he reached Cheriton Shawe.

He was in time to catch the four o'clock coach. When he got down at Wyminden Lane it was nearly five. He crossed the road and rang the bell of the first house he came to. He asked if there was any garage close by where he could hire a car. There was. He telephoned from a box at the next corner, and in less than five minutes he was speeding towards Cheriton Shawe.

When they came to the gateway, he asked the driver to wait for him. He stepped over the chain and took the short cut to the house across the lawn of the statues. He rang the bell. There seemed to be nobody at home. He rang again, and, after a further delay, the maid opened the door.

"You been ringing long, sir?" she asked. "I was just making ready to go home."

"I want to see Miss Meriden," he announced. "Is she in her studio?"

"No, sir. She's not here at all, sir."

"You mean she went back to London with the guests?"

"There's been no guests, sir. That's been put off like. Was she expecting to see you?"

"No, not exactly. Have you heard from her?"

"She rung up the Swan, sir, and the landlord sent my brother along with the message to say that nobody was coming and the mistress wouldn't be home."

"What does that mean?"

"She'll be staying in town tonight."

"At her Chelsea flat?"

"I suppose so, sir. She always stays at her flat."

"What time did she ring up?"

"Must have been about three, sir."

Andrew was worried. He had a feeling that something had gone wrong, that she was in trouble. "Listen, Gert," he said, "I came all the way from town to see her. It's important. Can you give me the address of the Chelsea flat?"

"Well, I don't know, sir."

"You mean you don't know where it is?"

"Yes. I go in to help Miss Meriden with the cleaning sometimes. I know where it is all right, but she's a bit particular."

He deliberated whether he would produce a pound note or not, and decided that it might be fatal. Gert gave an overwhelming impression of incorruptibility.

"It's very important, Gert," he urged. "You know I'm a friend. I was out here yesterday, remember?"

"I remember all right." Gert was dubious on only one point. "Are you sure Miss Meriden would like me to give you the address?"

"I'm sure she won't blame you. I'll guarantee it."

Somehow Andrew got the worried frown off his face and turned on one of his confident smiles. It always worked with patients. It worked with Gert.

"Oh, well," she said, "you did stay to lunch, so I suppose it's all right. The flat's at 18 Palgrave Street, top floor. The way I usually go, I take the tube to Sloane Square."

"Thanks. I know the street. I must hurry back to town."

He hurried. The coach from Wyminden Lane sped through gathering dusk, and lights were on along the route. At Oxford Circus he took to the tube and got out at Sloane Square. He found the house in Palgrave Street and rang Ruth Meriden's bell. No one came down the stairs to admit him. The house door was locked. He rang the bell again and worried whether it worked or not. It was an old house, and the bell buttons looked as if they had been there in the days when Franklin flew kites. The name plate opposite the button had been rubbed almost flat with much polishing so that you had to take an oblique view to read it in the flame of a match.

Once more he tried the bell. Then he went down the steps from the porch and out onto the roadway, and looked up. There were lights behind the blinds or curtains of all the windows except those on the top floor.

He fought down a feeling of panic. It was all right. He had come here merely to check the maid's story, but there was really no need to doubt its accuracy. She had gone to dinner with that American dealer. Or she was spending the evening with Hinckleigh. Probably she had stayed in town to spend the evening with Hinckleigh, and that was all there was to it. Why anyone should bother about a woman who could bring herself to spend an evening with Hinckleigh . . .

The door of the house opened as he teetered in indecision. A white-haired old lady, dressed for an Edwardian night out, came down the steps and was turning in the direction of King's Road when she saw him.

"Oh!" she exclaimed. "Have you been making all that infernal racket with the top-floor bell? Enough noise to wake the dead. What's the matter? Are the duns working overtime?"

"I'm sorry," he said. "I was anxious to get hold of Miss Meriden."

"High time somebody was." Her sweet little laugh made him want to strangle her. "That young girl is too serious; much too serious. It's no use your ringing that bell again. She isn't home."

"Do you know if it's long since she went out, madam?" Andrew's tone of high courtesy was marred by a slight tremor.

"About six weeks, I should say." The old lady laughed gleefully.

"Hasn't she been at the flat this evening?"

"She certainly has not. She wouldn't dream of arriving without letting me know."

"Perhaps she'll be getting in later. I'd better leave a note."

"That's right. You leave a note in the box. I'll look after it when I come home from the ballet."

She swung off abruptly with the sprightliness of a girl in her teens.

Andrew hesitated. Here his anxiety should end, because the danger, if any, would be at Walden House, not in town. In the morning he could send the girl a telegram asking her to telephone him. Or he might call at an early hour. So long as he warned her about the danger that might threaten her at Cheriton Shawe, his duty would be done.

He turned away in bitterness, thinking of Mr. Hinckleigh. He went to a pub on King's Road and had a drink. He was a little hungry then, but thought with loathing of a lonely dinner in an unknown café. He felt grubby, too, after the long day of running round to no purpose, and discontent accentuated the feeling till he believed he must look like a tramp. Impossible to think of eating before he had been home for a wash and a clean shirt.

A taxi took him across to Holland Park. There were limits beyond which economy became foolish even for a potential hospital registrar, and the limits were reached in his weariness and dejection.

He did feel a little better for the wash and the change, though, as he knotted his tie, it seemed to him that the Maclaren face had lost a lot of its buoyant air. It had a hunted look; and there was a dark puffiness under the eyes that no medical man could accept with equanimity, especially in the absence of compensating dissipation. He shook his head. A little of that dissipation would be good for him. Up to now this so-called holiday in London, this homecoming spree, had been a flop. Time he had a few drinks; time he announced himself to his friends; time he took a nice girl out to a good dinner. Who was Mr. Hinckleigh that he should have all the fun? Dr. Maclaren was not without resources. Indeed, no! Marilyn Webb, for instance. Lovely, witty, cheerful, and he'd get all the inside dope on the hospitals at the same time. But perhaps not tonight.

He went through the list of resources, and finally decided on Sophie Gaines, who was lovely, witty and cheerful, and didn't know a hospital from a hole in the ground. The best of the lot of them. He had always liked her. If he hadn't gone off on his Red Cross jaunt, who knows what might not have happened. A radiant girl, Sophie. She glowed.

It was singular, then, that he dialled her number without any responsive glow. As he swung his finger round the circle from the last cipher, he was more dejected than before. Only when he discovered that he had got on to a wrong number did he feel the slightest relief; but doggedly he began to dial again. As the mechanism whirred unhurriedly, the bell of the flat door rang loudly.

Eight . . . nine . . . He dialled the last two digits of Sophie's number, wondering about the caller at the door. An impertinence, walking up the stairs to the flat without so much as pushing the bell button at the front entrance to give one notice. Jordaens, probably. The police approach.

The automatic ringing-tone was calling Miss Gaines.

He held on. The caller on the door mat might, of course, be somebody for Lang; somebody accustomed to coming informally up the stairs. Or it could be Mr. Botten. After his experiences in M.I. something-or-other, Charley probably considered it undignified to bother about house bells when front doors were open.

Another imperious summons from the flat door cut through the transmitted ringing-tone of the telephone.

Andrew slammed the telephone down on the cradle and bounded from his chair. Then, as he touched the latch, another possibility occurred to him. The enemy had come back. Kretchmann, Haller, Mr. Jolly-Face, the man in the flapping raincoat. One or more of them, and the boss himself for choice. Andrew was in the mood, ready for him, a word of welcome on his lips.

He flung open the door and then jumped as if he had been shot. A flash of light made him close his eyes, but the flash was an inward experience, unseen. He opened his eyes and blinked as if the illumination had been actual. Ruth Meriden was still there on the threshold.

Ten

THE first thing he saw was that something had upset her very considerably, but even as he stood aside for her to come in, she burst out exasperatedly.

"Where have you been? I came here looking for you before. I phoned! I phoned and phoned! Where have you been?"

"Looking for you. You told me you were going home. I had to see you, so I went out there."

"To Cheriton Shawe?"

"Yes, but what on earth's happened to you?"

She limped past him into the room. There was a long scratch on her face and mud on her coat.

"I fell down," she said wearily. "And I think I'd like a brandy—"

Something in her tone stilled the questions crowding to his lips. He went to her quickly.

"Here, you'd better sit down. I'll get you something."

She sank into a chair exhaustedly. "I ought to have gone back to Palgrave Street," she said. "But like a fool I didn't. You see, I got frightened."

"Oh." He handed her a glass. "Don't sip it. Drink it right down."

She did, then gasped a little. He took the glass away and refilled it.

"What scratched your face?" he asked.

"A bramble."

'What about your leg?"

"I've bruised my knee. It's a bit stiff, that's all." He gave her the refilled glass. "You'd better sip that one."

"I shall be drunk."

"No, you won't. Do you feel like telling me what happened now?"

She nodded and then, to his relief, she smiled. "It was that wretched boat," she said. "I tried to find it for you."

"You did what?"

And then she told him.

Throughout the morning her thoughts had kept going to the boat. For that reason, perhaps, she had failed to take any interest in the American dealer and, in the end, had asked him to postpone his visit to Cheriton Shawe until his return from Paris a fortnight hence. She pleaded that she would then have more work to show him. They had argued about schedules and sailing dates with Mr. Hinckleigh, and finally it was agreed. Then Mr. Alec Foster bought them a good lunch. He was really a very nice person, and she liked him very much.

"But the boat?"

"I'm telling it just as it happened," she said. "After lunch I went to see the lawyer. He didn't know anything about the boat, but he remembered the mill." She paused. "It's a windmill," she said.

"A windmill!" With his knowledge of John Quayle Meriden's peculiarities, the information should not have been startling. He was surprised because he had visualised something else. A windmill did not seem to go with streams and landing stages. It was rather a thing of bleak uplands and windswept plains.

"Is it the mill we're looking for?" he asked.

"I don't know. It seems likely, from the position. I was too frightened to make certain."

"What do you mean?"

She said irritably: "Why did you go down to Cheriton Shawe this afternoon?"

"Never mind that now. Tell me about the mill."

It seemed that years ago Uncle John had gone duck shooting at Groper's Wade on the Thames Estuary and had returned in a state of high excitement about this windmill. He had recently read a magazine article on the production of electricity by wind power, and had been inspired by the idea. He would buy the ruined mill, restore it, equip it with a generating plant and demonstrate that the theories of the magazine writer were sound. Then he would buy up windmills all over the country and furnish enough cheap electricity to supply the nation's needs. The Meriden System would be the salvation of industry, and John Quayle would be honoured wherever a spark was required to turn a wheel or light the darkness.

"You find out who owns that mill," he had instructed the lawyer. "Get it for me cheap, and keep your mouth shut. Once my plan is known, the price of windmills will go up."

The lawyer had opened his mouth only to make objections, but Uncle John had remained firm. When he had heard the price, he had been delighted. He had never known anything so cheap, a bargain! The owner threw in the mill cottage, landing stage, all appurtenances, and riparian rights, if any. The agreement had been signed and the price paid. Within a week he had forgotten about it, and nobody had been inclined to remind him.

"That's what one might have expected," Ruth Meriden commented. "Do you know where Groper's Wade is?"

"Not exactly," Andrew confessed.

"You take the train to Britsea and then you walk across the marsh or fen or whatever you call it."

"All right. I'll go down tomorrow and explore." At the moment it did not seem so important. "What I want to know is how you got yourself into this state?"

"I went down to Britsea."

"You what?"

"I went down to Britsea," she repeated calmly. "I telephoned you here from the lawyer's office. I telephoned three times from different places. Then I decided to go down and check on the mill. I thought you'd like to know definitely if the yawl was there." "Good God!" he exclaimed. "You shouldn't have done that alone! Didn't you realise there was danger? After all I told you about my being shadowed?"

"I didn't think there'd be any danger to me."

"Look! I went out to Cheriton Shawe today because I wanted to bring you back to town. I was afraid for you, alone in that crazy house. I thought the gang who killed Kusitch might find the link and go after you. And you walk right into their hands. You're lucky to have got away from them. They might have killed you. Now that they've found the yawl, there's nothing more we can do. We'd better call up Scotland Yard at once and let the police clear things up."

"Will you stop being melodramatic and listen to me? I didn't walk into anybody's hands. And nobody has found the boat. At least, not as far as I know. When I got down to Britsea it was later than I expected," she said. "Have you any idea what Britsea's like?"

"Well, what *is* it like?"

"Hell," she said simply.

Britsea, it appeared, was a bungalow colony with a few Nissen huts added for architectural variety. It had a station. She had asked the solitary porter if there were a windmill and cottage in the neighbourhood, and he had pointed to the North Sea and said: "That would be Groper's Wade. First to the right past the garbage tip.

The lawyer had told her that it was a short walk to the mill, but when she came in sight of it, it seemed to be miles away—a squat stump on the edge of nowhere with dark clouds piling up behind it and the day looking as if it were going to do an early fade-out. It was cold, too. A wind blew in from the sea and across the marsh unhindered. She went on a little farther. Then she became afraid that she could not reach the mill and get back to the station before nightfall, and the idea of darkness on the marsh was not pleasant.

"Even in the daylight it's bad enough," she said. "The fact is, I wouldn't have gone on in any circumstances. I was scared of the loneliness. I can't stand it when I find myself in the middle of nothing. Then I got the idea I was being followed, and—well, I suppose I fell into a panic."

Andrew cut in with a question. "What gave you the idea? Did you see anyone?"

"Yes. A man was poking about in the garbage dump. There's a level, filled-in patch and the trucks tip their loads into the hollow. The man was by the edge of the hollow when I passed, poking about with a stick."

"He was there before you?"

"Yes, but he could have come on the train, except that I never noticed anyone like him at the station. I think I would have, because he was very tall and thin."

"Don't tell me! A tall thin man with a cloth cap and a long grey coat that flaps round his legs when he walks?"

"No. Nothing like it. He didn't have a hat or coat; just slacks and a rough sort of seaman's sweater."

Andrew let out a sigh of relief. "Just an old tramp," he decided. "You'll find one on every garbage dump, looking for bits of metal and other things that might bring in a few pence."

"That's what I thought," she agreed. "If you hadn't put this shadowing business into my head, I wouldn't have taken any notice. I didn't at first, but I happened to look back, and he'd come over the edge of the hollow and seemed to be watching me. That was the first thing that started me off. When I looked back a little later, he had disappeared. I told myself that it was all right, but it wasn't. I believed he might be following me to snatch my bag. Then I thought he might have something to do with the Kusitch business, and that was when I really panicked."

She paused a moment, not happy in the recollection of it. When she went on, she made him feel the strain of it.

It was pretty bad, she said. When she decided that she could not go on any farther, she found that she was too scared to go back.

Dusk was coming quickly across the marsh, or it may have been the lowering clouds. Already there were lights in some of the bungalows, and they seemed far away, unreachable. She took a step towards them, and halted. Thirty yards or so from her, she saw a dark movement behind the fringing reeds and rushes of a pool at the track's edge; a shadow diving for cover, but diving too late.

"I was paralysed. I just stood there, staring at the reeds, waiting."

All over the desolation were pools with screens of reeds and rushes, tall enough to hide a man bent double, and the track between the windmill and the station found a winding way among them.

For minutes she could not take her eyes off the spot where the shadow had vanished. Then her mind began to work again. She must go forward to the windmill, or back to the station. But there was no real alternative. The farther she went towards the windmill, the worse her position became. She must go back, must risk the danger that waited behind the screen of reeds. Perhaps there would be no challenge; perhaps the game of shadowing would go on. If the main purpose was to observe her movements, there could be no purpose in any interference. She had led the watcher nowhere. She had merely walked out into the middle of a wilderness; now she proposed to walk back again.

It took all her will power to make her legs move. Keeping her eyes focused on the reed screen, she went forward slowly. Every moment she expected the man to rise up and block her path, but nothing happened. The wind from the sea was behind her now, and gulls rode in on it, screaming and squawking. There was no other sound except the dry rustle of the reeds. She went on tiptoe, as if that might help her to pass the screen, and as she approached it she edged towards the far side of the track. She had a plan now. If the man waited a fraction too long, she might evade him. She could run. She selected the spot from which she would start. It was a little forward of the screen, and the turf on the side of the track was obviously firm enough for her to take an oblique course. That oblique course was essential for the first twenty yards or so. The track curved slightly, so she could gain an advantage.

She walked boldly now, with a pretence of ease. She reached the chosen spot and dashed off, leaving the track in her desperate race. Five yards, and her left foot caught in a trailing bramble. She crashed down, barking her knee on a stone and tearing her cheek on another bramble. As she fell, a wild bird rose from the screen of reeds and went off with a whir of dark wings.

"A bird!" she said. "A damn silly bird!"

Andrew made a sympathetic sound.

"I started to cry," she admitted. "I think it was rage more than anything else, but I was still frightened. I believe I was more frightened. I lay there on my face, crying, till I found I was partly in a pool of water. Then I got up and went on. I ran. I imagined a man was coming after me. I imagined a shadow behind every clump of reeds. It was all imagination. I should have gone on. I had time to get to the windmill and back. I might have found out about the boat."

"I'm glad you didn't," Andrew told her. "We'll go together in the morning. I'll hire a car and drive you."

"We'll have to leave it till the afternoon. I must go to the gallery in the morning. Hinckleigh is furious over the way I behaved today."

Something in her intonation took away all his animus against Hinckleigh. Besides, there was the way she had behaved today.

"All right," he said. "We'll leave it till the afternoon. Now we'll go and get something to eat."

"Like this?"

"You can tidy up here. Anyway, we'll go somewhere quiet."

"Well, if you don't mind . . ."

He decided on the restaurant where he had dined with Charley Botten two nights ago. It was an admirable place for the occasion. It was unpretentious, the food was excellent and the wine reasonable.

The only drawback was that Charley Botten used it regularly, and might well be there tonight. He liked Charley, he was even fond of his company at times, but on this occasion, no.

Andrew's anxiety was relieved in part as soon as he entered the place. Mr. Botten was there, but he had a companion, a grey-haired man, and they were already halfway through their dinner. When the headwaiter suggested a table on the other side of the room, Andrew raised no objection. Mr. Botten saw the newcomers and made a crouching rise, clutching his napkin, in acknowledgement of Andrew's nod.

"Somebody you know?" Miss Meriden inquired.

"A stockbroker," Andrew said.

She smiled across the table when they were seated, and Andrew was glad that the stockbroker had a companion. Possibly a client. Andrew glanced at the man but got nothing much more than the back view of a rather worn jacket that looked like a Harris tweed, badly cut and very creased. To judge from what could be seen, the man was of medium height and on the portly side. His grey hair, fluffed out round a bald spot, gave the effect of a monk's tonsure.

But Andrew gave him no more than a glance. Ruth Meriden had smiled and the promise of her smile was fulfilled. The meal was a success. Andrew never could recall afterwards exactly what they had talked about; all he ever knew was that they had both talked a great deal and that what they said had been trivial and light-hearted and yet, in some magical way, profoundly important. Then, as he turned to order coffee, he became aware of a movement on the other side of the room. He was conscious of Charley Botten again, and glanced round.

Charley and his guest had risen from their chairs. They came across the carpet to reach the central passage between the tables, Charley leading the way, his bulk obscuring the smaller man. He gestured vaguely in the direction of Andrew, something between a wave of farewell and a hiker's hitch-signal. An instant later Andrew saw the face of the fluffy-haired guest. He stared. There was no mistaking that affable, beaming countenance above the rough tweed fabric of the ill-cut jacket. Clap a hat over the high bald forehead, and all you needed was the jigging phrase from *Till Eulenspiegel* to make the picture complete. Charley Botten's guest was the supposed shadow, the *siffleur* of Holland Park, Mr. Jolly-Face himself. Andrew blinked, then laughed, turning to hide his laughter, but Jolly-Face had passed on towards the exit in the wake of his host.

Ruth said: "What's the matter?"

He had begun to tell her when Mr. Botten re-entered the room and came towards their table. He was by himself now.

"Hello, Andrew," he said. "Everything satisfactory? Are they treating you well?" He might have been the proprietor of the place, solicitous about the comfort of his clients. He canted the wine bottle and glanced at the label. "Not bad," he conceded. "The Volnay here is better though."

Andrew spoke without cordiality. "Miss Meriden, may I introduce Mr. Botten?"

"How do you do? I thought it must be Miss Meriden. I wanted to come across all the evening to meet you. Unfortunately I had to defer the pleasure on account of my guest."

"Isn't he waiting for you?" Andrew asked.

"No. I pushed him into a taxi."

"Who is he, by the way? I seem to know him."

"That's improbable. He's just a wartime colleague of mine. Hadn't seen him for years."

"I think he's living in my neighbourhood."

"Really?" Mr. Botten shrugged and felt vaguely in the pockets of his waistcoat. "He did give me his address. I put it in some pocket or other. Doesn't matter." He pulled up a chair. "May I join you for a moment?"

Andrew nodded coldly. Ruth was looking a little puzzled. Andrew explained Mr. Botten. He was not merely a stockbroker; he was the friend who had collected the facts about the boat.

"I want to ask about the mysterious yawl," Charley said. "Have you had any luck?"

"We think we've found it," Andrew informed him.

"That's nice. So Miss Meriden is co-operating. Where do you think you've found it?"

Andrew explained. He described, with the girl's assistance, the supposed location. Mr. Botten asked questions, and heard the de-tails of Ruth's misadventure. Then he wondered whether they were on the right track. Mr. Meriden had talked of a mill, not a windmill. The landing stage seemed to be the important clue, and, in Mr. Botten's view, landing stages didn't seem to chime with windmills. "Have you checked the spot on a large-scale map?" he inquired.

Andrew had no suspicion that Mr. Botten was moved by anything but innocent curiosity. He thought the large-scale map was rather a good idea. That was where M.I. experience came in.

"Miss Meriden didn't wait for maps. She dashed off to Britsea at once."

"Anyway, we'll know all about it tomorrow afternoon," Miss Meriden asserted cheerfully. "Andrew and I are going down by car."

Andrew's heart jumped. "Andrew and I"—it had a delightful sound.

"I'd have liked to go down with you," Mr. Botten said.

"Can't you?" Ruth asked.

"I'm afraid not," Mr. Botten lamented. "We've a lot on just now, and my partner's away. But you ought to check up on the map. If you know what you're going to find, it will be easier to find it. There's the matter of roads, too. Let's all go to my place for coffee, and we'll investigate."

Andrew managed to sound dispassionate. "I think after the day she's had, she ought to be in bed."

"Dr. Maclaren," the girl explained, "is treating me for a bruise."

"Then come along," Mr. Botten said playfully. "I'll open a bottle of vintage arnica."

Objection was useless. In half an hour they were in the Botten flat with coffee and liqueurs. The owner had a collection of maps most efficiently indexed. Groper's Wade was contained within a small section, but the scale was enormous.

"Here you are!" Mr. Botten pointed with a pencil. "Groper's Mill. The circle represents the mill structure, and here's the landing stage all right." The windmill was about a half mile inland, provided you gave the term "land" to the swampy reed beds that surrounded it. A creek wound in from the estuary—one of many creeks on the map—and close to the mill a small rectangle was drawn, jutting out from the bank into the narrow stream. The mill cottage was defined by a larger rectangle on the land side of the small circle.

"Nice map," Charley commented. "Shows everything except the yawl. Here's your road, Andrew. It must run parallel to the track you took, Ruth. There's only the one way across the swamp. Here's the station. Where would you place the garbage tip?"

Ruth took the map and indicated the place. Andrew frowned. He resented Mr. Botten's easy friendliness. He also resented the way she accepted it. He got up from his chair. It was time to go, but Mr. Botten had not finished. He was almost as bad as Inspector Jordaens in his passion for interrogation, and now his line was to suggest that Ruth might not have been entirely mistaken in thinking she had been watched. She insisted that she had been the victim of an overheated and infantile imagination.

"In the matter of the bird among the reeds, yes," Mr. Botten admitted, "but can you be quite sure about the man in the garbage tip?"

"I can be quite sure that he didn't follow me," Ruth answered.

"Yet you admit there was ample cover if he had wanted to use it?"

"I suppose so."

Mr. Botten was like a prosecuting counsel with a shifty witness.

"You say that this man could not have followed you from town because he was unlike any of the passengers who left the train with you at Britsea?"

"Yes."

"You base this assumption or conviction merely on the difference in dress?"

"Isn't that enough? The man was tall; there was only one tall man at the station, and he was wearing a hat and some kind of overcoat. He was in the middle of a group round the exit gate. I remember him because of his height. My recollection is that all the men from the train wore hats and coats. It was fairly chilly with the wind coming across the river flats."

"And the man in the garbage tip was in sweater and slacks?"

"Yes."

"Doesn't it occur to you that he might have taken off his hat and coat to deceive you?"

Andrew laughed. "Still on the old cloak-and-dagger stuff, Charley! Aren't you forgetting the false beard and the dark glasses? Are you sure, Ruth, the fellow didn't have a black patch over one eye?"

"I'm fairly sure he didn't leave the garbage tip," she said.

Mr. Botten was still suspicious. "He could have watched you from the hollow. He wouldn't have had to leave the tip." He turned to Andrew. "I wouldn't go down there tomorrow if I were you. I think you ought to leave it all to me."

"Leave it all . . . !" Andrew began indignantly and then swallowed his indignation. "We're ahead of the enemy, we're ahead of the police, and I'm not going to wait till they catch up with us. All this stuff about being followed is just nonsense. Why, the other night I believed I was being shadowed by the man you've just had as a dinner guest! Every time I notice a fellow in the street I think he's on my trail. Ruth's right. It's all imagination. I'm even beginning to have doubts about that Brussels business."

"And possibly there was no Kusitch," Charley suggested. "All right. I wash my hands of you." He grinned. "When you get the yawl in order, you may take me for a sail. My own opinion is that it was never brought back to England, but that's just, as I say, an opinion. It might be as well, though, if it were at the bottom of the sea."

"Why do you say that?"

"I don't know." Charley shrugged. "Put it down to a hunch. I don't like trouble. I never did. If the yawl's gone, there's no more harm in it. If it's tied up by that old windmill, heaven knows what sort of mess is going to come out of it."

"What could come out of it?" Mr. Botten considered the question for a moment. About to reply, he hesitated and spread his hands helplessly. He said: "I learned to suppress ideas about second sight during the war. If you want to call in a crystal-gazer, don't mind me. But there's one bit of advice I can give you without a crystal ball. Keep a sharp lookout when you're on the road tomorrow. If you're followed by a car, don't go anywhere near Groper's Wade. Just take a joy ride into the country and come back to town."

Andrew left Ruth at the door of the house in Palgrave Street. She said her knee felt better and she didn't need any help up the stairs. She had been silent and thoughtful in the taxi from Charley Botten's. On the doorstep she was practical.

"I shouldn't keep the cab waiting," she said. "I'll be ready at one o'clock. Good night."

On the way home and afterwards Charley's final piece of advice recurred to him. He believed it was pointless, yet it continued to worry him. How could the enemy, not knowing his plans, have a car ready to follow him? Charley, of course, had intended no more than a cautionary hint, and, as a precaution, he would take the hint. He would keep a sharp lookout.

Eleven

NO CAR followed them. He glanced frequently at the driving mirror of the small car he had hired, and Ruth kept a sharp lookout through the rear window. Passing through the outer suburbs, they had had some suspicion of a Citroën saloon, but this was resolved at a main road junction, and, when they ran out into the country and sped along a flat stretch, they became certain that, for the moment at any rate, their movements were not supervised.

The sky was overcast and there were omens of heavy weather far out in the estuary. The prophets had modified the threat of showers with a promise of bright intervals, but so far there had been neither showers nor bright intervals. Not a day for a joy ride. The sea, when they saw it across a tumble of dunes, was wan and melancholy under the dour spread of cloud, yet Andrew had not felt so happy in a long time, and Ruth seemed astonishingly carefree. Could he ever have thought her smug? Of course not. She was direct, friendly, gay. Andrew was happy to be beside her. He was happy to be driving a car in England again, and it mattered not at all that this particular England was a dreary area of sand and coarse grass and mud flats, of bleak bungalows and bleaker colonies of cylindrical oil tanks. It might have been the loveliest stretch of lakeland in sunshine or some glowing corner of the summery Chilterns. He had not been so happy since his return from Greece.

Not even the slough of Groper's Wade under a drizzle of rain could dampen his spirits. He saw its dreariness, the wide misty sweep of marsh that ran into the green-grey distance so that you could not tell where the sedge left off and the sea began. From the slight rise above Britsea Halt, the pools that dotted the waterlogged smudge were like filmed eyes turned blindly to the sky. But these things could not affect him. He was detached from all dreariness by a singular enchantment. He had only to turn his head to see the warm loveliness of the girl beside him.

He turned and saw her frowning.

"It's a horrible place," she said, and grimaced, shuddering.

"Your wounds must be troubling you." He laughed. "It's just a place. Nothing to worry us, anyway. We can be back at that nice cottage for afternoon tea."

The nice cottage was miles behind them, in another world. The road across Groper's Wade was defined by water-filled ruts that reflected the dull light in the overcast. There was no trace of the windmill ahead; only a featureless haze. Slush spouted from the wheels of a truck filled with junk for the rubbish tip. Andrew drew level and shouted to the driver, who brought his vehicle to a stop at the turn into the dump.

"How's the road across the marsh?" Andrew asked. "Is it safe?"

"Aye!" The reply rasped through the sound of the truck's revving engine. "Safe enough if you stick to it." The man grinned broadly. "Don't try any short cuts."

He was quite incurious. He let in his clutch and swung his load of junk into a sharp turn. Another man was standing in the entry to the tip, waving the driver to come on.

"Identify either of them?" Andrew asked Ruth.

She shook her head. "Neither is like the man I saw, but what does it matter?"

"Just wondering." He was still quite happy about it, but the marsh, now that they were actually upon it, started a germ of uneasiness in his mind. The panic of Ruth on her first visit was easy to understand. The place was fertile ground for any seed of fear. It might even generate fear.

Ruth pointed to the side of the track. "That's where I fell down," she said. He stopped the car and got out.

He asked: "Is that the bunch of reeds where the bird was?"

"Yes."

He was cautious, crossing the spongy ground on the edge of the road. Even after the rain there might be footprints. A man crouching would drive his heels or toes deeply into the turf, and it was not likely they would be soon eliminated. The ground wasn't that spongy.

"What are you looking for?" the girl asked. "You don't think a wild bird would have stayed in among those reeds with a man hiding alongside?"

"It was just an idea," he said. "The bird might have been flushed from another clump. In the twilight you might not have seen clearly."

She shivered but made no other reply.

The drizzle had stopped, but the sky looked as watery as the earth and the sea. Far away you could just make out the shaft of the windmill and the roof of the adjacent cottage.

"No wonder you were scared," he said.

He went back to his seat and drove on slowly. The rutted track seemed solid enough. It was the same rain-washed drab green that stretched away on both sides of it, but under the short tough grass it was a made road. Stone and rubble and road metal had been packed down to make a causeway. Someone had made a thorough job of it in the days of cheap labour and material, and it had lasted. But he still drove slowly. There might be a fault somewhere, and it would be no fun getting stranded with a hired car.

Then, indistinctly in the distance, they saw the mill.

They both peered forward through the windscreen, eager for the details that gradually became apparent as they approached. The windmill was like a grey monolith perched on a small knoll with a tumble of low dunes behind it. The monolith grew into an octagonal tower with a domelike cap, and the skeleton remains of the sail-frames, the four long whips or arms, became visible. There had once been a paved yard between the mill and the cottage, but most of the stones had been entirely covered by the coarse grass. Andrew advanced the car gingerly into this space, and backed and turned before pulling up.

The girl moved to get out, but he restrained her. They kept their seats for a moment, listening. There was a sound of wind and the squeaking complaint of corroded metal as the arms of the mill shuddered and swung a little. Nothing else.

Now the two stepped out and stood gazing up at the mill. It was a massive structure when you came close to it. The arms must have measured thirty feet from axis to tip, but they were dead arms, except for that slight shuddering movement that caused the metallic sounds. They would hang on the landward side till they rotted away. The vane that had once been there to rotate the cap and bring the sails to the wind had long since gone. Windows were dark, boarded-up slots. There was a heavy, weather-bleached door. It was shut.

They looked at the cottage—a simple two-storeyed affair in an advanced state of dilapidation. Here the door had fallen in, the windowpanes had been broken, the roof had a hole in it.

"This doesn't look as if that will add much to the value of the estate," Ruth said. "Let's go."

"In a minute or two." Andrew grasped her arm and guided her across the yard and round the knoll of the mill.

"Why are you tiptoeing?" the girl asked.

He grinned. "It's the marsh again. Listen!"

The grinding creak of the mill's rusted mechanism was followed by the low moan of a dying wind. The sea swished and murmured and hung in silence between the waves. Far off the whistle of a locomotive sounded.

Ruth and Andrew moved on round the mill, and there, before them, were the winding creek and the landing stage.

And there, too, was the boat.

The two masts of the craft swung slowly from side to side as the hull yielded to the tidal movement in the creek. Weather-stained, battered, her peeling paint stained with rust, you wondered that she was still sound enough to keep afloat.

Ruefully, the girl stared at her. Then she laughed.

"There's your prize," she said. "A nice reward for all the trouble and worry. She's yours, Andrew. I make you a present of her. What do we do now? Go home?"

The yawl swung round a little with the movement of the water and they could see, showing faintly through the Calabrian fisherman's casual effort to over paint them, the words on her square stern: TENDER TO MOONLIGHT.

Andrew shook his head. "She's got something to tell us: why Kusitch started for England to find her, why he was murdered in Brussels, why . . ." He broke off. "Anyway, let's look at her."

The berth was snug. There was a wide bend in the creek like a small cove, sheltered on the seaward side by the low dunes; on the other side, by the knoll and the windmill and the cottage. The craft was secured by an anchor and a mooring buoy; also she was made fast to the landing stage by a steel cable with sufficient slack to take care of the rise and fall of the tide. And there were rope fenders to protect her if she were forced against the timbers. At the moment there was a clearance of about a yard, and the deck was a few inches below the level of the landing stage, a platform of heavy planks projecting four feet over the water.

Neglect of the paintwork was even more apparent on closer inspection. The hot sun of the Mediterranean had dried out the oils and whitened the woodwork. Paint had peeled and scaled away, but one could still make out the registration number on the bows, SS 729, showing through the over paint applied at Zavrana.

No doubt Ernest Jansen had done his best to bed her down safely after her voyage home from Bova Marina. Sail covers had been lashed in position and everything left shipshape, but now a roughly folded tarpaulin lay on the deck, forward of the coach roof. Andrew stared at it uneasily.

Plainly that tarpaulin had covered the open well of the craft; clearly it had been removed quite recently—today, or yesterday. From the landing stage no other signs of interference could be seen, but Andrew found his uneasiness increasing as he stepped down onto the deck and reached out a hand to his companion.

"Now we're on board," she said, "what do we search for and where do we search?"

They stood in the well of the craft and looked round. The auxiliary engine had a teak housing secured by a padlock. At least there was the appearance of security, but, when Andrew tested the padlock, he found that a hack saw had been used on it, and a slight tug brought the hinged part of the lock away from the staple fixed to the housing. He told himself that his worst fears might be unjustified. A deserted craft was an irresistible attraction to marauding boys or petty thieves. Parts of an engine could be removed, sold to a junk dealer, used. But when he lifted the cover of the housing, the engine seemed to have been cleaned quite recently. The magneto looked particularly bright, and might have been placed in position that day.

He thought about the magneto. An experienced man like Ernest Jansen, knowing that the craft would be tied up for months if not years, would never have left it there. The engine housing might be sound and well constructed, but the moist sea air would penetrate at various points, and moist sea air was bad for magnetos. One either took them ashore or stowed them in a more protected place. Andrew was no sailor, but he knew that much.

"What does it mean?" Ruth asked, sensing his apprehension.

"I don't know."

He stood up and looked round, but knoll and windmill hid the track across Groper's Wade. Above the marsh gulls wheeled, crying raucously, swooping and rising again. There was more light under the overcast, and the gulls were paper-white against the dark cloud. Beyond the dunes, rain squalls slanted across the sea.

Ruth climbed onto the deck, stepped ashore, and mounted the

knoll.

"Not a soul in sight," she announced, "if that's what's bothering you." He nodded. He could feel and smell the emptiness. He could smell something else, too. He went down on his haunches beside the engine and sniffed. Paraffin, and newly poured. Someone had been using paraffin to clean the engine. He picked up a cigarette end and examined it. It had not been there very long.

Ruth came down to the landing stage. "What have you found?" she asked.

He threw the butt into the creek. "Doesn't mean a thing," he commented. "Someone has been taking an interest in her, that's all. It's a miracle she hasn't been looted before this. Your Uncle John should have had more sense. I'm going to take a look inside."

Ruth came on board again.

The padlock of the sliding companion hatch had been treated in the same way as that on the engine housing. In addition a fitted lock had been forced with a chisel or similar tool. Andrew opened the hatch and led the way below deck. There was a miniature galley on one side of the entrance, a small pantry or storeroom on the other side. Both were completely empty, stripped of whatever fittings they had once contained.

Beyond was a fairly roomy saloon with a chart table in the centre and bunks on either side. A door forward gave access to a small water closet, and right forward, divided from this cubicle by a wooden partition with a sliding panel, was the usual chain locker. There were fitted drawers for clothes under the bunks, and one of them contained a piece of old blanket, a piece of oilskin, and a length of string; more evidence that Ernest Jansen had been thorough in preparing for the lay-up, for it was plain enough that here the magneto had been wrapped and stowed.

The wrappings were the sole find. The saloon, like the galley and pantry, had been stripped. Once, no doubt, there had been mattresses and cushions but at some time, in Dalmatian or Calabrian waters, someone had gone through the craft and left only the bare boards. Was it rational, then, to suppose that anything of value remained in the yawl?

Andrew peered into corners, resisting the thought of the anticlimax that now seemed inevitable. But it was difficult to resist with much conviction. He was a fool, and must appear doubly a fool in the eyes of Ruth Meriden. Kusitch had thrown away his life in pursuit of a myth. Kretchmann and Haller had committed murder for nothing and embarked on a futile errand. The treasure coveted by Kusitch and his assassins had vanished. Whatever it was, a booty of jewels or a priceless old master, someone had removed it. Unless there was some secret hiding place in the craft. As well expect to find a hiding place in a matchbox.

"If there ever was anything, we're too late," Ruth said.

She was thinking that Kretchmann and Haller might have preceded them by a few hours, even an hour. The possibility was not to be dismissed, but if Kretchmann and Haller were the interlopers, why had they taken the magneto from the saloon drawer and fitted it to the engine?

Andrew went forward and opened the panel of the chain locker, but it was empty except for some rusty anchor chain. He rapped on timbers and looked behind the drawers. There were no secret cavities that he could discover.

Ruth had returned to the well to watch the wheeling sea gulls. Perhaps she had been merely curious about the yawl, for she showed no sign of disappointment. Andrew imagined that there was even a hint of secret amusement in her smile when he emerged from the saloon and shrugged his shoulders.

She said: "If the masts were hollow, you could hide a few Rembrandts in them."

He grinned but a trifle sheepishly. She climbed ashore again and watched him from the landing stage, while he rummaged among fragments of canvas and broken tools and other odds and ends in the sail lockers.

"While you do that," she said after a moment, "I'm going to take a look at my new cottage. It may be full of Persian miniatures or Aztec birdbaths."

Andrew looked after her gloomily as she limped up the knoll. The implied criticism may have been aimed at the late Uncle John, but it could have had another target. This hypothetical treasure of the tender to *Moonlight* must seem absurd to her now, but it had been real enough to Kusitch.

Somewhere in this shabby tub there was or had been something, but Andrew could think of no further place where he might search. If there were a concealed cache, an unsuspected space behind an undiscovered bulkhead, he did not know what he could do about it short of ripping the craft to pieces. He looked up at the solemn heavens, but they just went on being solemn. He looked down at the rust-marked, oil-stained boards on which he stood, and they were but little more inspiring. He observed, but without conscious intention, how neatly they were fitted together to make a floor; how each board had a finger hole for ease in lifting. An idea came to him, but when he translated it into action it was with no eagerness.

He lifted one of the boards from the bilge stringer and detached it from its ledge on the middle bearer. He lifted a second board, but he was already convinced that no one would have hidden an art treasure in such a place. The wash of water in the bilge was filthy with grease and drippings of oil from the engine. Ribs, strakes and keelson were smeared with something that looked like tar, and the heavy slabs of metal that served as ballast had been daubed with the stuff. He tapped one of the bars with a screwdriver from a locker. Pig iron.

Rocking in the slow swirl of the bilge was a tin can with part of a bright new label attached.

If he had not observed it, he might not have realised that someone had been bailing out the bilge, though the little depth of water in the bottom should have told him that at once. Since Jansen tied up the craft, the bilge would have filled with water in one way or another. The fact that it had been bailed out linked up with the curious business of the magneto. Some sort of overhaul had been attempted. The floor boards had been removed to get at the propeller shafting and coupling.

Andrew gazed down at the dark water and the iron pigs for a moment. Then he replaced the floor boards and closed the companion hatch, putting the padlock back as he had found it. He saw then that the deck was almost level with the landing stage and the tide was still running in.

Ruth called from the knoll, "There's a man coming along on a bike."

One of the local inhabitants, no doubt! Might even be a coast guard or something. Possibly he would know if anyone had been nosing round the yawl in the last few days.

Andrew stepped ashore and climbed the knoll to Ruth's side. The man was pedalling slowly across the wade, taking the bumps, weaving and twisting in his course to avoid the worst of the depressions in the track. Andrew watched without suspicion until he saw that the burden of a two-gallon petrol tin was adding to the cyclist's difficulties. The fact was too peculiar not to be taken as a warning. If the tin contained petrol, the fellow's objective must be the yawl. At once the other peculiarities fell into line: the sawn padlocks, the cigarette end, the magneto.

At that moment the cyclist saw them. No doubt he also saw the car in the yard. He came on without hesitation, quite confidently, as if he knew his way about.

Andrew gripped Ruth by one arm. "Don't say anything," he told her. "Leave it to me."

She turned to smile. The smile said clearly: "Oh, come now!"

"We must find out what he's up to," Andrew added in justification. "I'll bet he's been messing around with that engine."

"If he's that interested, maybe we can sell him the whole thing."

The man was about forty-five. He had a hard, weather-tanned face and fairish grizzled hair. He wore toil-marked grey slacks and an old brown jacket over a dark green sweater. He dismounted and leaned the bike against the mill. He was cheerful and friendly, with a proprietorial assurance. He put an empty pipe in his mouth.

"Afternoon," he said. "Come out to see the mill?"

"That's it," Andrew agreed. "I suppose it's quite noted."

"I suppose." The man nodded and grinned, jumped into the well of the yawl, and began to pour the petrol into the fuel tank aft. Andrew and Ruth followed to the landing stage and watched him.

"What do you think you're doing with that craft?" Andrew inquired, forcing back his indignation.

"Making her work," came the affable reply. "Owner's instructions. Mr. Robison says make her work. So, I make her work."

Having disposed of the petrol, he uncovered the engine, fussed with the carburettor for a moment, then swung the starting handle.

There was no result.

"Is Mr. Robison the owner?" Andrew asked.

"No, he's the boss." The fellow looked up for a moment. "Bad state this engine's in! Bad! Know you anything about them?"

"Not much. Do you?"

"Nothing I don't know." He swung on the handle again, and again there was no result. "Looks like real trouble. Maybe the plugs." He frowned, taking it hardly. His heart was in his work.

"Who's Mr. Robison?" Andrew persisted, ignoring an attempt by Ruth to draw him from the landing stage.

"I told you who he is." The mechanic was less affable. "He has a garage, if you wish to know."

"In Britsea?"

"Along the London road."

"Who's the owner of the craft?"

"That's not my business." The mechanic straightened himself. "And it's not yours. This is private property. You have no rights here. You wish to look at the windmill, no one is going to object." He took his pipe out of his mouth.

141

Ruth whispered: "For heaven's sake, let's go."

Andrew stepped in front of her and glared down at the mechanic.

"I'm well aware it's private property," he snapped. "It belongs to this lady; all of it—the mill, the cottage, the yawl. What's more, she hasn't ordered any repairs by Mr. Robison or anybody else. You can leave the engine alone. Now get out of that craft and take yourself off, before I bring the police here."

The man reached down and picked up a broken hammer from the sail locker. He stepped onto the deck and faced Andrew menacingly. For a moment he looked dangerous; then he changed back to the affable mechanic and smiled a slightly bewildered smile. He put his pipe back in his mouth.

"There must be a mistake," he said, "though how that can be, I cannot explain. Mr. Robison is not usually confused. The craft by the windmill, he said to me, and there's no other windmill here nor another craft. You talk to Mr. Robison. He'll be here any minute. Promised to give me a hand with the engine because the owner's in such a hurry. Quiet at the garage, we are, so Mr. Robison . . ." He broke off as he turned to look towards the track across the marsh from the slight elevation of the deck. "See, he's coming now!" he said. "You can speak."

The newcomer, like his mechanic, had a bike, but instead of riding he was wheeling it and balancing a jerrican on frame and handlebars. He was a tall man in an overlong grey raincoat, and he had a cloth cap pulled down over his eyes. When he leaned the bike against the wall of the mill and lifted the jerrican from it, he was obviously lifting the full weight of petrol. He came down the knoll with the long grey coat flapping against his legs, and Andrew saw that under it he was wearing slacks and a seaman's sweater of rough blue wool.

Pieces of the puzzle were beginning to fit together, and Andrew had bitter thoughts as he looked upon them. He had been right after all to suspect the man in the long coat. He had been followed to the

Blandish Gallery the day before. He had led the man to Ruth
Meriden and she had been trailed to Groper's Wade. And Charley
Botten had been right in his theory about the tramp in the rubbish
dump. It was very easy to remove one's hat and coat and hide them
for a moment or two, and, hatless and coatless, anyone might be
mistaken for a local inhabitant. This fellow had watched Ruth start
on her way across the marsh, and the direction she took had been
clue enough for him. He had waited for her to return. Then, no
doubt, he had started to explore. Once the yawl had been found, he
and his mechanic had lost no time. Andrew stared into the dark
deep-set eyes that had focused on the Dufy in the window of the
Blandish Gallery, and once more he had an odd feeling of familiarity,
a sense of having seen the man somewhere else in different
circumstances.

The mechanic said: "I'm glad you have come, Mr. Robison.
These two people are trying to make trouble. The man claims that
the woman owns the craft we have instructions to repair. I have told
him there must be some mistake. Perhaps you will be able to
straighten the matter out."

"By all means let us straighten the matter out." The newcomer
put down the jerrican on the edge of the landing stage. "We need to
speak plain without making fictions. The Dr. Maclaren knows there
is no mistake. So, I think, does the Fräulein Meriden. Before I have
had only the distant pleasure to see you, gracious Fräulein."

He touched his cap and made a slight bow, and in that moment
of mocking gesture the sharp ferret like features of a face that had
the immobility of a ventriloquist's dummy were fully revealed.
Andrew knew him. The chambermaid at the Risler-Moircy had
called him Herr Schlegel. He had waited that morning in Brussels to
inspect the suite from which Kusitch had been taken in the night.
Now the dark eyes that were the living part of the face had the same
evil assurance.

"The Herr Doktor and I have met once before," he said. "He
showed kindness to me. He left in the room of the man Kusitch an

empty envelope. When I find an empty envelope, I have the conviction there may have been something in it. I hope the Herr Doktor will continue to co-operate." He turned to address the mechanic. "I believe that will be his best policy—best for himself, best for the gracious Fräulein. What do you think, Haller?"

Twelve

SCHLEGEL, Robison! There might be many other aliases, but they would all add up to Kretchmann and Haller— Inspector Jordaens' friends. And that meant. . .

Andrew checked his thoughts. This was not the moment for internal argument. It was equally futile to abuse himself for his folly in exposing Ruth to danger. Now, as Haller, with a smile, stepped from the deck of the yawl onto the landing stage, Andrew retreated a step from Kretchmann and drew the girl towards him with an arm round her. His one thought was to protect her, but, even as he made the gesture, he realised its stupidity. He needed both arms free at this moment. The tactical possibilities were limited. First he must knock Haller into the creek with one well directed blow; then he must batter Kretchmann to an insensible pulp. Child's play for the conventional hero, but he was not a conventional hero. He doubted his ability to execute even the first part of the programme.

"For myself," Kretchmann said, "I am always agreeable to co-operate. I am full of the friendliness and peace when people are reasonable. I hope the gracious Fräulein is reasonable. She has, I think, not so much interest in this little boat. On the other hand, my friend and I have the great need for it, to make a journey. It is not our wish to steal, only to borrow. Somewhere or other your property will be found and returned to you, Fräulein. Meanwhile, you and the Herr Doktor will be able to take up residence in your cottage. I hope you had a hearty meal at midday, because I am afraid we have no supplies to leave you. But perhaps the police will find you."

"You can't lock us up in that place," Ruth protested.

"Oh yes. It is certain," Kretchmann said in his dead voice. "The necessity is to be regrettable, but I can see no alternative. What do you think, Haller?"

"Kill them," said Haller. "We don't want witnesses."

"My friend learned his English from a London war prisoner. He speaks like the native," Kretchmann asserted. "He loves the English very fondly, but he has little patience. He is interested only in our journey. We shall leave this evening."

"Why do you want the craft?" Andrew demanded. "If you think there's anything of value in it, you're wrong."

"You have searched?" Kretchmann managed to contort the lower part of his face into a smirk of amusement. "Kusitch told you something, but are you sure he told you enough?"

"I'm sure someone has been here before you." Andrew released his hold on Ruth and moved an inch or two away from her. While facing Kretchmann, he was watching Haller, waiting for the moment when the man would be off guard. "There's nothing in the craft," he insisted.

"Then there is no reason why you should object if we take a little trip in it."

"I do object. It is Miss Meriden's property. You've no right to move it."

"Perhaps the gracious Fräulein will not be so difficult. I do not care for difficult people. That was the great fault in your friend Kusitch."

"Talk will never make the engine work." The impatient Haller turned to Kretchmann as he made his protest, and that was Andrew's moment. He hurled himself forward, putting all his weight into a blow that would topple the man into the creek. But Haller was not there to receive the blow. Before Andrew could recover his balance something hit him with sickening force in the back of the neck. He sprawled forward helplessly and saw a boot coming up to meet his face. It grazed the side of his head, but there was sufficient force in the impact to stun him. Through a mist of pain he heard Ruth cry out. Then the boot drew back again. There was a moment of terror; then a light blazed in his head and he felt himself sinking.

He was in darkness and his body was in some peculiar and excruciating state of tension. Through a kind of singing in his ears he could hear faint fluttering sounds. He opened his eyes and there were thin parallel strips of light like white rulings on a sheet of black paper. He stirred and then gasped as he was shaken by a wave of pain.

"Andrew."

The voice came very softly from the darkness somewhere near him.

"Andrew. Are you all right? Andrew."

Consciousness was making its way back slowly and uncertainly, like an insect seeking a way of escape through a window.

"Andrew."

He was beginning to remember now. She was somewhere near him. He tried to speak but the sound he made was a kind of gasp.

"Andrew."

Suddenly he began to cough; and even as the throbbing agony of it tore through his head he came to his senses. He was lying on a bare wood floor and his hands and feet were bound, the hands behind him and tied to the rope round his ankles.

"Andrew. Are you all right?"

For a moment he lay there gasping for breath. Then he licked his lips.

"I think so. Are you?"

"Yes, but I can't move."

"Where are we?"

"In the cottage by the mill."

"Where are our friends?"

"I heard them arguing over the boat. They couldn't get the engine to start. I caught odd words. I think they've gone to the garage at Britsea for something. Are you sure you're all right?"

"I don't think there's anything broken. How long have they been gone?"

"About five minutes."

"Did they take the car?"

"No."

There was a pause. A kind of numb lethargy was stealing over his body, abating the cramp in his legs and arms. Soon, perhaps, it would soothe the pain in his head and he would sink back into a blessed unconsciousness. Then, in the silence, he heard her catch her breath in a sob.

The sound acted like an alarm signal, jolting him back into an awareness of their predicament. Unconsciousness now could mean death—for them both. He opened his eyes again to the strips of light showing between the boards nailed over the window. Then he tried to move his hands. The rope was round his wrists and his fingers were nowhere near the knots. It was good rope too, thin but as hard as whipcord.

"Ruth."

He heard the effort at self-control she made before she answered.

"Yes?"

"Whereabouts are the knots?"

"There aren't any. They used ropes from the boat with metal eyes and tied the ends with wire."

His heart sank but he persisted. "Could I untie the wire with my fingers?"

"I don't think so. It's thick wire. It took the two of them to twist it."

It would have to be the rope then. A faint hope suddenly flickered. "Did they search me?"

"Yes. They wanted to see if you had a pistol."

"Did they empty all my pockets?"

"I don't know."

"Did they take my lighter?"

"I don't know." "If they didn't, it's in a ticket pocket inside the right-hand pocket of my jacket. Can you move far enough to see if it's there?"

"I'll try."

He heard her feet scraping along the floor seeking a hold. A moment or two later she rolled over against him. Her hands were by his chest.

"Hold on."

With an effort he edged backwards and then rolled over on his face. He felt her hands against his hip.

"It's there. Keep still."

There was a sudden movement and then he heard the lighter clatter on the floor.

"I've got it."

He rolled over again. A moment later the lighter clicked and he could see her lying with her back towards him, the lighter held up between her fingers.

The first glance told him that it would be impossible either to untwist the wire with his hands or to burn through the rope about her wrists; the wire was of stranded steel, rusty but still tough; the rope was too near her wrists at every point to be burnt without also burning the flesh. He had another idea.

"Can you stand the lighter on the floor without putting the flame out?"

"I think so."

It was difficult for her and she burned her hands doing it, but she managed in the end. He remembered thankfully that he had filled the lighter the previous day. It burned steadily as he rolled on to his back and manoeuvred the rope about his ankles into the flame.

The rope began to char almost at once but so did the material of his trouser legs and he had to keep pausing in his efforts and hold his legs away from the flame. By the time the rope parted and his ankles were free he was almost too exhausted to stand up.

The next thing was to free his hands. The lighter flame was low now and he knew that he had to move quickly to find something against which he could abrade the rope between his wrists.

The only thing that presented itself was the rusty bracket of an old shelf. He found that he could just reach the curved brace of the bracket before the light went. He began to saw at the rope.

There was no doubt about its being good rope. He worked away in an exhausted silence. The girl spoke only once.

"Can you do it?"

"I think so."

It took nearly half an hour and his wrists were bleeding when it was done but, although he was aware of pain, it seemed to him now that his nerves no longer responded to it.

Steady movement of the bracket had loosened the screws that fastened it to the wall. He wrenched it off and with it prised open one of the windows sufficiently to admit a working light. Then, using the bracket as a lever, he tackled the wire cable that secured the girl's hands.

At first he scratched his hands and tore his fingernails, but once he could use the leverage of the bracket his task became easier. She was almost free when suddenly he felt her stiffen.

"What is it?"

"Listen. Didn't you hear it?"

"Hear what?"

"They're back! They're at the car! I heard the door close."

The blood was thumping so in his head that he could hear little else. He said, "They'll make for the yawl. We'll hear them talking."

They listened. There were sea gulls and silence.

Andrew went to the window again. No one was visible. The craft swam high, but the tide was past the full.

"You could have been mistaken," he said.

"I tell you I heard the car door."

"All right. Hold still now." The last knot came free and he helped her to her feet. She sat down again with a groan as the circulation began to return to her limbs. Andrew went back to the window. Yawl and landing stage were still deserted. It might still be possible to reach the car and drive off, but caution was imperative, for by now Kretchmann and Haller must be on their way back. The essential thing was to reach the car and start it up; then a couple of encumbered cyclists would have no chance against them, especially if they were taken by surprise just outside the yard.

The bracket had one more job to do. Andrew tried the door and found that, although there was only a simple latch on it, it had been jammed in some way from the outside. There was, however, a crack in one of the door panels and he set to work with the bracket. It bent and finally broke but he had done enough damage to the panel to enable him to get his arm through and remove the piece of wood wedged in the latch. They went out on to the landing. Then they stood still for a moment, listening anxiously, but there was no sound. Even the gulls were silent now.

"Wait here," Andrew said. "I'll look around first."

From the window of the opposite room he could see the yard and the car.

"There's no one there," he said. "We'd better not waste any time."

"Please be careful." She grasped his arm again. "I'm sure I heard someone at the car."

He was recovering now. "We'll both be careful," he said.

She followed him nervously. When a stair creaked under his weight, she started and caught her breath. They went on down quickly to the plaster-strewn floor of the hall.

"Andrew!" They were close to the open doorway of the cottage when she called to him in a whisper of apprehension.

This time there could be no doubt about the noise. He heard it himself. A man coughed. Then footsteps sounded in the yard, approaching from the rear of the cottage. Andrew opened a door on his left, pushed Ruth ahead of him into the room, and closed the door again. He saw dimly, between the slats of a broken Venetian blind, the figure of a man. What he saw was enough to tell him that the man was neither Kretchmann nor Haller.

"It must be another of them," he whispered to Ruth. "If he goes upstairs, we'll make a dash for the car." "He might come in here."

There was one possible hiding place, a cupboard on one side of the fireplace. The shelves had been removed, the doors swung on broken hinges.

Andrew shook his head when Ruth pointed to it.

"If he comes in here, I'll tackle him," he said.

"He may have a gun." She was trembling now. He could feel it through the hand resting on his arm.

"All right," he said.

They crouched together in the cupboard. He tried to close the doors; they would not meet, but the gap was narrow enough. They waited, trying to control the sound of their breathing. The man seemed to be in no hurry. He had paused on the doorstep. He was still looking round outside.

They crouched there painfully, listening. The footsteps sounded again—this time on the littered floor of the hall passage. Then the room door opened, and, Andrew, peering through the gap between the cupboard doors, saw a hand advance with a finger ready on the trigger of an automatic pistol.

Except for a portion of fawn raincoat, the rest of the man was masked by the room door, and almost at once the door was closed again. The fellow had seen an empty room, and that had been enough for him. As he crossed the hall to the other front room, he began to whistle faintly, allaying his own anxiety. He whistled as he went along the hall and climbed the stairs, and the tune took shape, became identifiable.

It was the rhythmic, jigging phrase from *Till Eulenspiegel*.

Thirteen

ANDREW'S HEAD SWAM. He felt as if he had been kicked in the head again. Then, after the first shock, he had a new fear. Vague at first, like something seen in the far distance, it rushed upon him with the speed of an express train. He could not evade it. He was tied to the line. The train passed over him and swept on, leaving the clatter of a name in his head.

Charley Botten.

He shook his head, fighting off the implications. Mr. Jolly-Face and Charley Botten, the two of them at dinner last night, the departure of the guest, Botten's return, his keen interest in Groper's Wade, the pinpointing of the large-scale map . . .

But no, it was impossible! He had known Charley Botten for years. And, anyway, this was no moment to bother about him. There were other things to think of, and little time to act. When Mr. Jolly-Face found that the prisoners had flown, he would stop whistling *Till Eulenspiegel*.

Andrew forced his mind to deal in practicalities. "When we get to the car," he said, "climb in the back and keep down on the floor. It will be safer if that bird starts shooting."

"What about you?" she whispered.

"I'll keep my head down. I don't expect he could hit anything with that thing anyway." He grasped her arm and pulled her towards the door. "Come on now, quick!"

They ran for it, but no bullets poured from the side window

upstairs. Mr. Jolly-Face must have been in one of the other rooms. Ruth flung herself down in the back of the car. Andrew leaped into the driving seat, his hand reaching for the starter button. He was about to press it when a shock of despair paralysed him. He had left the ignition key in the instrument panel. It wasn't there any longer.

"What's the matter?" the girl demanded breathlessly.

"It's no good. They've taken the key."

He spoke dully, inwardly cursing himself. Had it been his own car he would have been more cautious; had he come upon anything but a seemingly empty wilderness, he might have remembered, before he left the car, that the key was where the garage hand had placed it for him. Even with the arrival of Haller and Kretchmann he had failed to think of the key.

"What do we do now?" Incredibly, it seemed to him, the girl still looked to him for help, and all he could do was sit there behind the wheel in a kind of daze. He could neither think nor move. In cramped suspense he awaited release, and found it quickly in the sound of a petrol can bumping on the handlebars of a bike. He looked through the windscreen and saw Kretchmann and Haller returning across the marsh.

He crouched down along the front seat. The car was a good enough hiding place for a moment or two, but they must find something better and quickly. To run for it was out of the question. The way was too exposed. If they were seen, they would have two armed men after them; and Haller, also, might be armed. Kretchmann, for one, would think nothing of shooting them.

"Keep down," he said, "but get ready to go."

"We can't go back to the cottage," she said.

He knew it. If he had anything in mind it was that they should make for the cover of the dunes beyond the cottage. Once the alarm was given, the three might disperse in a frantic search for the fugitives. If this happened there might be a slender chance of escape, how slender he did not dare to think.

Surely, by now, Jolly-Face had discovered their flight from the room upstairs. The broken door on the landing and the rope must have made the truth immediately apparent, and it was a little puzzling that he did not hurry down to take action, even if he had not yet realised that Kretchmann and Haller were back.

Andrew waited, head raised so that he could just see the door of the cottage.

At last the man emerged, still holding his automatic waist-high in front of him but with a vague abstracted look on his face; as if, under his breath, he was still trying to improvise something on the theme from *Till Eulenspiegel*. For a moment he paused and looked round him in a puzzled way. Either he did not care that the prisoners had escaped or he knew nothing of them. Then, suddenly, he turned and walked away in the direction of the sand dunes.

Andrew thought quickly. The dunes were no longer a possibility. They could not stay indefinitely in the car. The only alternative was the windmill.

He didn't like it. They might simply be rushing from one trap into another. Besides, the door might not open. It could be locked or nailed up. But where else could they go? They would just have to take a chance. The enemy was pressed for time. They must sail at nightfall.

"We'll try the mill," he whispered.

"When?"

"I'll give the word."

Kretchmann and Haller were close by now. The dull *clunking* sound of the full petrol tin against the bicycle grew louder and faded. Then after a moment or two there was the faint tinkling of a spanner on a cylinder block.

Now, while the two were concentrating on the engine, was the time to move.

"Now," he said.

Andrew got out of the car and closed the door soundlessly. Ruth followed him.

They ran to the wall of the cottage, then halted for a moment.

Haller was swinging the starting handle of the engine now. The engine fired once and then died. Andrew pressed Ruth's arm and they went stealthily round the corner and along the front of the cottage, then ran the few remaining yards to their objective.

In the last split second the question posed by the closed door seemed an enormity, so fateful that Andrew was afraid to grasp the handle, yet there could be no hesitation. He gripped and turned and pushed, and the door would not budge. He thrust with a shoulder, and it yielded, swinging in on creaking hinges.

The relief was almost painful. He pushed Ruth through the opening, followed her, and closed the door slowly and quietly. His need now was for something with which to barricade the door, but, in the first moments, the darkness inside the mill seemed impenetrable. They waited, straining to accustom their eyes to the gloom. They were afraid to move because of possible obstructions and hazards of collapsed flooring or open traps. After a while they saw that there was a little light. Slats had rotted and broken away from the boarded windows, and the day seeped in through the gaps.

They moved in from the doorway, testing the floor and finding it sound. Great rectangular shapes loomed in the heavy dusk, barring the way, and there were voices uttering inarticulate sounds of warning. Inside this place the grinding metallic noise caused by the shifting sail-frames was magnified enormously, and a hundred creaking and screeching overtones came down from the cap on the top of the structure to join in an eerie concert. The wind that blew gently from the sea was an orchestra in this sounding-tower, running a dynamic scale from a whisper of flutes to a gusty percussion, and sometimes there was a sound almost like a human cry for help.

Andrew felt the girl's hand on his arm. He pressed it with a reassurance he did not feel, then got his lighter out. The warmth of his body might have evaporated enough fuel for a momentary flame. The flame lasted three seconds, but in that time the rectangular shapes took a third dimension and became great wooden bins. A small square of dim light showed in the low ceiling and Andrew saw steps ascending. He began to drag one of the heavy bins towards the door, but a new sound, distinctive, standing out against the background concert, made him wheel. The hinges creaked. He drew Ruth closer towards him, and they both saw the door open; saw the figure of a man in the slot of light; saw the door close again.

"The steps!" Andrew whispered. "We must climb to the next floor."

They moved silently. Then the beam of a torch cut across the darkness and travelled round the chamber. The two dropped down behind one of the bins. The beam travelled past them and was switched off. They waited. They heard no sound from the man, but they knew he was there with his automatic pistol held in front of him, guarding the door. A pause, and he came towards them. He bumped against one of the bins, but did not use his torch again.

Andrew looked up at the square of dim light in the ceiling. The steps were there, only a few feet from them. The noises of the place would cover any sound they made. He touched Ruth's hand, and she followed him, keeping close as he slowly proceeded, feeling his way cautiously, wary of obstacles. There was another long bin to conceal them, but when they reached the steps they were without any cover. He explored them quickly with his hand.

"There's no rail," he whispered. "Be careful, and go quickly."

He was suspicious, fearing that the torch might spear through the darkness and pin them on that fixed ladder, but it did not happen. They reached the floor above without mishap, and, in a few seconds, had lowered a trap door into position and silently moved a heavy bin on top of it.

There was more light on this floor, more gaps in the boarding of the windows, and they could see where they were. The bins were smaller than those below, and on one side was a small milling machine that had been worked by a driving belt from the next floor. A series of chutes also came down from the next floor, but Andrew was interested only in the tactical possibilities. They might ascend to the main grinding floors, and go higher still, past the great stones that had once pulverised the grain, till they reached the cap with its shafts and cranks and cogwheels.

They peered up into the tower through the open trap above and heard the noises of the mill in louder concert. They were nearer the source of the creaking and groaning, and also it seemed that the wind from the sea was getting up a bit. The mill was more restive, straining as if it wanted to set its sails going again and its great stones turning.

Ruth said: "If we have to go up there, I'm going to surrender."

"We'll stay here," Andrew promised her. There had been no movement of the bin, no attempt to lift the barrier, but this fact was not reassuring to Ruth.

"We're bottled up," she said. "If they don't make that engine work, we may be here all night."

"What about Charley Botten?" he said.

"What, indeed?" she answered grimly. "That's his friend downstairs, isn't it?"

Andrew was silent. He looked through a chink in one of the windows, but all he could see was the empty stretch of Groper's Wade. The afternoon was dying gloomily. It would soon be time for the yawl to push off if Kretchmann was to fulfil his plan.

He crossed to the opposite window and from there he could see the craft. Kretchmann and Haller were still working on the engine. They had been doing something to the magneto and were now replacing it. Haller was reaching down, working with a screw wrench. Kretchmann was fitting a lead from the distributor, to a sparking plug. When they had everything ready, Haller swung the starting handle, but the only improvement was that the engine gave an extra cough before it spluttered into silence. Haller swung the handle again and again, but it was hopeless, and by now they both knew it.

They talked in German. Andrew strained to hear, but failed to catch a word. Kretchmann gestured widely, pointing to the sky, then waving towards the cottage. Haller nodded, but seemed reluctant about something. The tide was running out now, and Kretchmann had to step up onto the landing stage. He walked up the knoll and disappeared, and a moment later the sound of an engine revving came from the yard. Ruth, sitting on one of the bins in deep dejection, raised her head.

"What's that?" she asked.

"That's our car," he answered. "It was Kretchmann who had the key. I think the yawl has beaten them. They're going to run away."

The diagnosis was reasonably correct, but Kretchmann had not yet finished with the yawl. When Andrew looked again through his spy hole, the German was backing the car slowly down the knoll to bring it to the edge of the landing stage.

What happened next made Andrew rub his eyes. He took another look, then beckoned to Ruth.

"What's the matter?" she asked.

"I'd like to know," he answered. "Either they're mad or I am. They're taking the ballast out of the yawl and loading it into the back of the car. Pig iron."

She stood beside him, peering through the gap in the boards. She saw the two men straining as they lifted the heavy bars of metal onto the landing stage and then into the car. Another, and another, and another . . . smeared with some black substance, filthy with oil and grease. They were careless of dirt; they were eager, concentrating on the job, heedless of everything but that grim-looking cargo.

"Pig iron," Ruth said. "Pig iron!"

Then down the knoll walked Jolly-Face, still following the pointing muzzle of his automatic. When he was three yards from the car he called out something that the wind blew away from Andrew, but Kretchmann and Haller heard it, and Kretchmann turned as if he had been hit by a bolt of lightning. Jolly-Face raised his pistol and aimed it at Kretchmann's head and Kretchmann and

Haller lifted their hands up and reached high.

Jolly-Face motioned sharply with his gun and shouted something. Andrew caught enough of the German to make out the whole of it. Kretchmann and Haller were to keep their hands high and get back in the boat.

Kretchmann objected: "What are you going to do with us?" "You have no need to worry. I am not going to turn you adrift. The car—" Andrew missed what was said about the car, but heard something of what followed. "You will be extradited, no doubt. Belgian . . . looking for you . . . Kusitch."

Kretchmann argued sharply. "You can't hold us. You've no warrant."

"This will do for a warrant." Jolly-Face gestured with his pistol. "I will bring you the English police. With them you may discuss warrants. Meanwhile you will rest in the saloon of your treasure craft. March!"

The plump little man and Charley Botten! Wartime colleague! So that was it!

Andrew stood up.

The little man had the controlling hand only so long as he kept the pistol pointed and his finger on the trigger. He was one against two, and Kretchmann was cunning, resourceful and ruthless.

Kretchmann continued to argue. His purpose was clear. He was trying to distract Jolly-Face's attention.

Andrew ran to the trap door, dragged away the impeding bin, pulled up the barrier and picked up a hunk of wood.

"Stay where you are!" he shouted at Ruth, and he had no thought but that she would obey him as he ran down the steps and blundered across the lower floor to the door. He heard her call after him but did not pause to answer. Jolly-Face was on his side, and the enemy were cornered. With the odds evened up, they could secure their prisoners. One could stay and make sure that they did not break out of the cabin while the other went for the police. But the first essential was to get Kretchmann's gun away from him.

As he came round the mill, Andrew knew he was too late. Haller was already in the well of the craft. Kretchmann sprang to join him, and as he landed appeared to stumble. He waved his hands as if to keep his balance, then fell forward. When he straightened up his revolver was in his hand.

Running down the knoll, Andrew heard the first shot. He crouched, getting the car between himself and Kretchmann, but Kretchmann, possessed, saw only the man in front of him. But he fired four times before Jolly-Face jerked back on his heels, then pitched forward on his face and began to crawl towards the landing stage, dragging himself with insect movements nearer to the killer. The little man was like a crushed beetle and as harmless, for his unused pistol had gone spinning out of his hand. Kretchmann sprang from the well of the yawl onto the deck and fired again twice at the crawling man. Andrew left the cover of the car and dashed towards the landing stage. He was as safe in that moment as he might have been in a tank, for Kretchmann hadn't seen him. But Haller had and scrambled from the yawl to meet him. Haller was eager, too eager. His foot slipped from under him as he touched ground. For an instant he was down on his knees; then, from the starting posture of a runner, he hurled himself forward. Andrew, in the moment of advantage, swung his club and caught Haller on the head. He saw the man spin and topple and fall back into the well of the yawl, but before he could lift his club again he took a blow on his own head from the butt of Kretchmann's empty revolver.

For a fraction of a second his mind was a blank. He must have closed his eyes. When he opened them again, he was struggling with Kretchmann, clawing and punching. His club was gone. He had only his hands, and his one thought was to avoid a second blow from the butt of the revolver. Wrestling, they reeled onto the landing stage, but by some miracle they stopped short of pitching into the creek. As they turned in frantic scuffle, Andrew caught a glimpse of the fallen Jolly-Face on the edge of the creek. The little man was motionless now. He lay prone with his head on one side and his face a smother of blood. Andrew was borne past him as Kretchmann made an effort. The two were off the landing stage. Then they tripped and, falling together, rolled in the sand.

Andrew broke away and got to his feet. Kretchmann had lost the revolver now, and came at him with wild, slugging blows, making him retreat. Then Kretchmann's left fist landed fairly, and Andrew went down, dazed and hurt and convinced that his jaw was broken; convinced, too, that the end would be brief and cruel. Kretchmann's boots would break his body, or Kretchmann's revolver butt would batter his brains out.

But none of these things happened. Panting, almost breathless, Kretchmann moved towards the car. Andrew dragged himself round and lifted his hammering head to look. The picture was hazy, as though his eyes wanted co-ordination. Then it sprang into sharp definition, and he struggled to his feet to face a new fear.

Ruth was there. She had come down the knoll from the mill and stood in the path of the killer. She bent down, reaching for something on the ground. The effect of casualness in the movement gave fantasy to the horror in Andrew's mind. She might have been recovering a fallen penny or picking a buttercup, but when she rose again she had the automatic pistol in her hand and a finger on the trigger. She pointed it, but Kretchmann leaped at her and brushed her aside with a sweeping blow. He was reckless of death now. Perhaps he disbelieved in it. Twice the pistol had been dashed from a threatening hand, and he was alive, going forward. He threw no glance at the girl on the ground, nor was he to be detained by any thought of the unconscious Haller in the well of the yawl. He got into the car, started the engine, and drove slowly up the knoll and past the windmill.

Andrew ran to the girl the moment she fell, but she was picking herself up before he reached her.

"Ruth!" he called. "Ruth, are you hurt?"

"I'm all right," she answered. "Get the car! The pistol!"

He saw the automatic in a clump of grass, and sprang for it. He ran up the knoll and took aim at the rear wheels of the retreating car. Kretchmann, driving slowly as if the springs were unsafe, was still within range. Andrew was a good shot with a pistol. He was confident when he pulled the trigger. He pulled it a second time. Nothing happened. The magazine was empty. It had not been loaded.

Kretchmann was out on the marsh, still driving slowly. The day had faded into dusk and lights were coming on in the bungalows round Britsea Halt. Kretchmann would soon have the cover of night, but the police would send out an alarm if the stolen car was reported.

Leaning against the windmill were the battered bikes that had been hired or purchased.

Andrew looked round. He must take care of his wounded ally and find out if Haller was alive or dead. Ruth would have to go to Britsea Halt and telephone. . . .

Ruth was kneeling beside Jolly-Face.

Kretchmann, halfway to the faint smudge that was the garbage tip, pushed on. Suddenly, from behind the smudge, a pair of headlamps glared along the track and came forward in haste. The lights picked up the stolen car, and it was obvious then that there would be no room to pass on the track. Kretchmann pulled up. He knew what was coming while Andrew still wondered. He left the car and ran for it, and Andrew saw other figures running, giving chase. There was little choice of direction for the fugitive. He ran back towards the creek, thinking, perhaps, that he might reach the dunes behind the mill, but when Andrew sped along the track to head him off, he turned across the marsh. The end, then, was inevitable. He floundered into a deep pool, and the pursuers hauled him out, a dripping prisoner.

Inspector Jordaens was the first to speak. "So, Dr. Maclaren, we find that you do not stop at theories. It is fortunate that we arrived in time, or Kretchmann would have slipped through our hands. As it is, we have lost Haller."

"You've lost nothing," Andrew retorted. "Haller is waiting for you. I—I looked after him. How did you get here?"

Jordaens was mollified. He almost produced a smile. "I do not quite understand it myself," he confessed. "You must ask your friend Mr. Botten."

Charley Botten was hurrying along the track, panting a little.

"Thank heaven you're all right," he told Andrew. "Where's Ruth? Safe, I hope?"

He took Andrew's assurance with relief, and went on. "I feel it's all my fault for letting you come out here. I got very worried. I began to think of that man in the garbage dump. I tried to raise Nimcik at his hotel, and he wasn't there. I suspected last night that he was in England because of the Kusitch business. He told me he had a clue to some lost loot. I didn't want to say anything about him till you'd seen this fishing craft. After lunch I got more and more worried. Finally I couldn't stand it any longer. I called up Detective Sergeant Stock." Charley paused for breath. "It was just as well we went over that map last night. We didn't have to lose any time." He paused again. "I suppose you haven't seen anything of Nimcik?"

Andrew composed a question, but did not ask it. He knew who Nimcik was. He said: "I'm afraid it's not so good. He tackled Kretchmann and Haller with an empty pistol."

Charley nodded. "I've heard him say a gun is a handy weapon till it's fired. He wouldn't want any trouble with foreign police."

"He's in trouble anyway. Kretchmann shot him."

They went over the knoll and down to the landing stage. Nimcik was sitting up, with Ruth supporting him.

"He'll have to go to hospital quickly," she said. "The one in the head looks like a scalp wound but there's another in the shoulder.

Not too serious but he's losing a lot of blood."

Detective-Sergeant Stock came over the knoll in a hurry. He was obviously excited. He looked bewildered, too.

"What's the meaning of it all?" he demanded. "Do you know what's in the car that Kretchmann was driving?"

Andrew, attending to Mr. Jolly-Face, looked up.

"Pig iron," he said. "They took it from the yawl. Pig-iron ballast."

"Pig iron!" Stock exclaimed. "It's bar gold! The car's full of gold!"

Mr. Jolly-Face smiled faintly. "Gold," he said. "A hundred thousand pounds worth of gold. It is now a matter for my legation."

Inspector Jordaens came from the yawl, having assured himself that the still dazed Haller was safe. He stooped near the edge of the landing stage and picked up an object from the sand.

"This is what I want," he asserted. "The revolver that shot Kusitch. One little test with the microscope, and my case is complete. Did someone say something about gold?"

Fourteen

MR. MILAN NIMCIK, of the Yugoslav Special Investigation Bureau, said a lot about gold, as, propped up in a hospital bed, he talked to his old colleague, Mr. Botten, and to his new friends.

The story began during the two weeks' campaign that shattered Yugoslavia in the spring of 1941. The Nazis poured across the northern frontier, flooding towards Lyublyana and Zagreb and Belgrade. They struck at the capital from Romania, too, and swept from Bulgaria into the Vardar Valley. They rushed on towards the Albanian frontier, they branched down towards Salonika in the south. Other forces engulfed Nish and Skopje. In six days Germans and Italians met at Struga, and the Yugoslav armies were divided and scattered.

Then there was chaos for the people. The fierce wind of the Wermracht tossed and whirled them all ways, and riding the storm came Kretchmann, a Feldwebel in charge of a small armoured reconnaissance patrol.

He was far out on the right flank of a motorised infantry division; his mission was to prevent the destruction of bridges and culverts on the transverse roads, and to feel for enemy forces reported to be reorganising to the north. He did not pause when the second vehicle in his patrol fell back with engine trouble. He had two motorcyclists and two men with him in the scout car, and that was plenty for the job in hand, even if there should prove to be some fight left in the local forces. Somewhere, in a patch of wooded

166

country, they ran across a fleeing van. It was not an army vehicle, just a delivery van with a baker's sign on the side of it, but it was important enough to have an escort of motorcyclists in uniform, and there was an officer on the seat beside the civilian driver. Here was transport commandeered in a moment of great urgency to carry something of high significance away from the invaders,—military secrets, plans, archives. Or treasure.

By then, Kretchmann and his men were trigger-happy. They shot up the van and the escort, and only one of the outriders got away. Kretchmann had a picked crew with him. They understood one another, and they understood their Feldwebel. Their wartime philosophy could be summarised in the word "loot," and they had it in mind as they inspected the van. They lifted an old tarpaulin that had been thrown in a heap on the floor of the van. There wasn't much under it; only seven great bars of gold.

Gold! The five men stared at one another. It was fabulous, a fortune. Not in all their dreams had they dared to conceive of anything like this. If they could get away with it, they would be rich. After the war they would live in comfort. To the victor, the spoils.

Kretchmann was the first to recover from the gratifying shock of discovery.

"It must be hidden," he said.

It was a thought in the minds of all of them: to make it safe so that they might claim it for themselves when the opportunity occurred.

First they must push on; put distance between them and the scene of the incident. Eventually they would report a breakdown in their radio on the command network, but not for some time.

They transferred the gold to the scout car and rushed on. They were excited, and perhaps a sight of the Adriatic from the high hills suggested wild ideas of desertion. Perhaps they just went blindly on, to see what might be round the next corner.

Nightfall was near when they descended to the little port of

Zavrana and came upon a small craft tied up to the pier of a re-pairing yard, a yawl with the strange English title of "Tender to *Moonlight."*

Zavrana appeared to be almost deserted. Yet they waited for darkness, their vehicles concealed in an olive grove above the town. When they felt it to be safe, they carried their treasure on board the yawl. They saw all the auspices as favourable. Fate had tumbled a fortune into their laps and had then produced a craft to carry them away.

They were ready to cast off when the beam of a searchlight swung in from the sea and travelled over the port. Other beams cut through the darkness, sweeping sea and shore, and Kretchmann knew that the plan was hopeless. Vessels of the Italian fleet were on the prowl, watching for fugitive craft.

"We must go back," he said. "In a few days the war will be over. We will be an army of occupation. Then we shall decide what to do."

"Let us bury the gold on shore," a man named Haller suggested.

"There's no time," Kretchmann objected. "Other units may be here any minute. If they catch us, we'll lose everything, and maybe our lives as well."

He took up the floor boards of the craft and inspected the ballast in the bilge. He raised seven pigs of iron and cast them overboard and replaced them with the bars of gold. Next he brought some tar from the yard and smeared it over the ingots and the remaining pigs of iron.

As he replaced the flooring, he said: "There's our hiding place! The gold couldn't be safer anywhere."

"Fine," Haller answered him. "What if someone runs away with the craft?"

"We shall come back before that can happen. Now there is no time for more."

Haller was not satisfied. He removed the magneto and threw it into the harbour. He took a hammer and smashed parts of the engine. "That will make it safer," he said, "but we must get back here very soon."

"Don't worry," Kretchmann told him. "It will be easy."

It was not easy. It was impossible. The Italians took over the occupation of the coast, and Kretchmann and his accomplices were sent to fight in North Africa.

"The next chapter," Mr. Nimcik said, "does not begin till after the war, when we began to investigate cases of looting with the object of recovering our national treasures. And this is where Kusitch comes into the story, a clever man in some ways, a fool in others. You will understand there were all sorts of papers to examine and among those that came to the desk of Kusitch was a deposition made by the surviving motorcyclist of the gold convoy."

Kusitch became very interested in the lost ingots. He could find no record of their receipt in the available German documents and he began to suspect the raiding party had made away with the gold. He established the spot where the incident had occurred. He mapped alternative courses that the looters might have pursued, and one of them led to Zavrana.

Here he found confirmation. A terrified boy, hiding from the invaders, had seen the Germans board a small craft, remain in it for some time, knock the engine about, then drive off again. The boat builder had fled in the general panic that had overtaken Zavrana, but when things settled down he had returned to look after his business. It was true that the engine of the small craft had been knocked about; moreover, the Germans had stolen the magneto. The boat builder restored everything, because he had made a bargain with the owner of the craft, a crazy Englishman named Meriden, who had left it with him for his use, provided he kept it in repair.

But there was small profit in it for the boat builder, for no sooner had he got the craft in working order than a group of Italian deserters ran off with it.

Here was an end to the trail, but Kusitch was not one to despair. "When I examined his correspondence," said Mr. Nimcik, "it be-came clear that he had used official facilities to make inquiries in Italy. There were many references to a yawl called 'Tender to *Moonlight*,' but most of them were negative. No trace, inquiries without result, not in this locality, and so on. No doubt Kusitch would have had ready an answer about some art treasure had he been questioned, but the strange references remained unnoticed until after he took flight from Athens. That was when I became busy, and the files finally told me that the yawl had turned up in Calabria and that it had been restored to its English owner at some time after the war.

"And there was another angle to investigate," Mr. Nimcik continued. "Just before Kusitch vanished, two Germans appeared in Zavrana and made inquiries about the yawl. We learned afterwards that one of them followed Kusitch to Athens, and it is obvious that this fellow must have warned Kretchmann about the fugitive's movements. We were keeping an eye on the other German as a matter of routine, so when I needed him, it was an easy matter to have him brought in as a suspected spy."

Mr. Nimcik smiled benignly. "I asked him a lot of questions," he went on. "Many questions. He was frightened. Finally he confessed. A man named Schilling, he was; one of Kretchmann's crew in the scout car. Not a nice man, though not so tough as Kretchmann or Haller; not, at any rate, as a single spy. He told me everything about the attack on the convoy and what followed. He told me that since the war their one thought had been to find the lost yawl, and Kretchmann had sent him to Zavrana with his companion to make inquiries. At Zavrana they had heard about Kusitch and his questions, and so they had watched Kusitch."

It seemed, then, that the destination of Kusitch had pointed the way to England for Kretchmann and Haller. They had intended to pick up Kusitch on the last stage of his flight and deal with him in England, but the grounding of the London plane had made them change their plan. These two might maintain a stubborn silence to the end, but speculation could fill in the gaps. They had seized Kusitch. They had tried to get from him the whereabouts of the yawl, but this was something that Kusitch himself had not known. His hope, it appeared, had been to get in touch with Miss Meriden, to tell her some tale, or perhaps to buy the yawl from her. He had known of her visit to Dubrovnik, had followed her to Athens and Brussels. Perhaps he had intended to spy out the land in England before approaching her; perhaps he had had the idea that she might lead him to the yawl. He had refused to say anything about these things, and neither torture nor threats had budged him.

"Kusitch was that type of man," Mr. Nimcik commented. "It was the Slav in him. Us Slavs are like mules sometimes, except that we have less feeling than mules. He would think: 'This Kretchmann believes I have the information, so he will never kill me.' But I have seen something of Kretchmann today. He is a man of violence, of sudden storms. He has the madness of the killer, and it is easy for him to press a trigger when he is in the anger of frustration. ... So the body of Kusitch is found in the Bois du Cambre, and by this time I am already in Brussels."

The benign smile of Mr. Nimcik travelled over the company and was directed at Andrew Maclaren. "And now the interest is focused on Dr. Maclaren, the companion and accomplice of Kusitch. Kretchmann is sure that Dr. Maclaren knows everything. I am inclined to be suspicious myself. The scene shifts to London. I watch Dr. Maclaren in the hope of picking up Kretchmann. Kretchmann gives him attention in the hope of discovering the yawl, and we know now that he is ultimately led to Miss Meriden. That was yesterday, but I was quite unaware of the young lady's visit to Groper's Wade. When I checked up on Dr. Maclaren, I knew that he could not have been in the confidence of Kusitch, so I dropped my interest in him. I had, you see, another line of inquiry, and it was productive. It was productive just in time."

Mr. Nimcik had caused an agent to investigate the Calabrian clue in the correspondence of Kusitch. This agent had found the fisherman of Bova Marina and had learned about the man Ernest Jansen who had claimed the yawl on behalf of Meriden. Jansen had spoken of his plan to migrate to Algiers. The resourceful Mr. Nimcik had inquiries made in Algiers, only to learn that Jansen and his wife had returned to England, disgusted with the climate of North Africa.

"It is, perhaps, no place for the Norseman," Mr. Nimcik observed. "The hot wind is hard on pink skin, but it blew me some luck, for Jansen was in London and this morning I located him, with the help of a private detective."

Inspector Jordaens uttered a grunt of disapprobation, but no one took any notice; not even Detective Sergeant Stock.

"With a little prompting"—Mr. Nimcik rubbed his thumb and forefinger together roguishly—"Jansen became informative. He told me about the windmill and the landing stage and the boat, and it seemed to me then that I was at the end of my mission. All I had to do was go down to Groper's Wade and make sure of the gold."

Charley Botten complained. "If you had confided in me last night, we might have co-operated. You told me a cock-and-bull story about a Cellini sauceboat."

"A diplomatic story, my dear friend," Mr. Nimcik protested. "If you had not been so uninformative when I asked you about Dr. Maclaren, I might have talked of a fishing craft instead of a sauceboat. It was because Dr. Maclaren was in touch with you that I sought you out."

"To pump me?" Charley laughed. "Was that your idea?"

"I was uncertain of my ground."

"You are a cunning old man."

"A foolish old man." Nimcik smiled his broadest smile. "I trust too much to my empty pistol. Not that a loaded one would serve me any better. If I stood on the doorstep I could not hit a house."

Inspector Jordaens was put out. "It is no matter for a joke," he protested. "You knew that Kretchmann and Haller were very dangerous men."

"I thought I was ahead of them, my dear Inspector," Nimcik answered. "After my talk with Jansen, I went down to Groper's Wade. As soon as I saw the boat, I knew that the others were ahead of me. I behaved with caution. I reconnoitred everything in the best possible style. I would have waited with patience to inform the excellent Scotland Yard, but I saw that Kretchmann and Haller were about to leave with the gold. I had no alternative but to interfere, to do my best. Fortunately it all ended well. You arrived in time to help the old man out of his difficulty, and now the work is done. My legation has been informed. It will be proved to the satisfaction of the British Government that the gold belongs to Yugoslavia. I believe the idea will be to use it for trade with this country, but the whole problem is one for the higher levels. For me, I would like now to sleep if you will not think me impolite."

Andrew took Ruth Meriden back to London in the hired car. It was very late when they reached her place in Chelsea once more.

He said: "I suppose you'll be going back to work tomorrow?"

"Not tomorrow," she answered. "I think I'll take a holiday."

"What about your work?"

"Work?" she said vaguely.

"What about Mr. Hinckleigh?" he went on. "What about Mr. Alec Foster?"

"I think they can wait," she answered thoughtfully. "When do you join that hospital?"

"I've three weeks yet," he told her. "We could, of course, get a special licence."

"And someone to repair the boat. We could fit her out and call her *Moonlight* and go cruising. Perhaps we'd find some more gold in her."

"What would we want with gold?" asked Andrew.

ERIC AMBLER

Doctor Frigo
ISBN: 978-07551-1761-1

A coup d'etat in a Caribbean state causes a political storm in the region and even the seemingly impassive and impersonal Doctor Castillo, nicknamed Doctor Frigo, cannot escape the consequences. As things heat up, Frigo finds that both his profession and life are horribly at risk.

'As subtle, clever and complex as always' - Sunday Telegraph
'The book is a triumph' - Sunday Times

Judgment on Deltchev
ISBN: 978-07551-1762-8

Foster is hired to cover the trial of Deltchev, who is accused of treason for allegedly being a member of the sinister and secretive Brotherhood and preparing a plot to assassinate the head of state whilst President of the Agrarian Socialist Party and member of the Provisional Government. It is assumed to be a show trial, but when Foster encounters Madame Deltchev the plot thickens, with his and other lives in danger ....

'The maestro is back again, with all his sinister magic intact' - The New York Times

The Maras Affair
ISBN: 978-07551-1764-2

(Ambler originally writing as Eliot Reed with Charles Rodda)
Charles Burton, journalist, cannot get work past Iron Curtain censors and knows he should leave the country. However, he is in love with his secretary, Anna Maras, and she is in danger. Then the President is assassinated and one of Burton's office workers is found dead. He decides to smuggle Anna out of the country, but her reluctance impedes him, as does being sought by secret police and counter-revolutionaries alike.

ERIC AMBLER

The Schirmer Inheritance
ISBN: 978-07551-1765-9

Former bomber pilot George Carey becomes a lawyer and his first job with a Philadelphia firm looks tedious - he is asked to read through a large quantity of files to ensure nothing has been missed in an inheritance case where there is no traceable heir. His discoveries, however, lead to unforeseen adventures and real danger in post war Greece.

'Ambler towers over most of his newer imitators' - Los Angeles Times
'Ambler may well be the best writer of suspense stories .. He is the master craftsman' - Life

Topkapi (The Light of Day)
ISBN: 978-07551-1768-0

Arthur Simpson is a petty thief who is discovered stealing from a hotel room. His victim, however, turns out to be a criminal in a league well above his own and Simpson is blackmailed into smuggling arms into Turkey for use in a major jewel robbery. The Turkish police, however, discover the arms and he is further 'blackmailed' by them into spying on the 'gang' - or must rot in a Turkish jail. However, agreeing to help brings even greater danger ....

'Ambler is incapable of writing a dull paragraph' - The Sunday Times

ERIC AMBLER

Siege at the Villa Lipp (Send No More Roses)

ISBN: 978-07551-1766-6

Professor Krom believes Paul Firman, alias Oberholzer, is one of those criminals who keep a low profile and are just too clever to get caught. Firman, rich and somewhat shady, agrees to be interviewed in his villa on the French Riviera. But events take an unexpected turn and perhaps there is even someone else artfully hiding in the deep background?

'One of Ambler's most ambitious and best' - The Observer
'Ambler has done it again ... deliciously plausible' - The Guardian

The Levanter

ISBN: 978-07551-1763-5

Michael Howell lives the good life in Syria, just three years after the six day war. He has several highly profitable business interests and an Italian office manager who is also his mistress. However, the discovery that his factories are being used as a base by the Palestine Action Force changes everything - he is in extreme danger with nowhere to run ...

'The foremost thriller writer of our time' - Sunday Times
'Our greatest thriller writer' - Graham Greene

Printed in Great Britain
by Amazon